Dimitris Leventis

Stories of *Famagusta*

NATIONAL PRIZE FOR LITERATURE · CYPRUS 2015

Armida Publications is a member of the
Independent Publishers Guild (UK),
and a member of the Independent Book Publishers Association (USA)

www.armidabooks.com | Great Literature. One Book At A Time.

Summary:
Stories of Famagusta is a collection of short stories that trace aspects of the life
of Famagusta. Even though most of the characters featured in the stories are
fictional, they represent inhabitants of the now Turkish-occupied Famagusta,
where no Greek has resided since August 1974.

The walls and harbour of Famagusta, its sandy beach with the lilies of-the-shore,
the promenade, the orange orchards, taverns, schoolboys and schoolgirls,
boy scouts, EOKA fighters, the war, friendships and animosities with the Turks,
love affairs, emigration, and the lives of refugees are all interwoven
into the fabric of the narratives.

The stories span the years from before World War II to the present day,
as the city lives on wherever there are Famagustans.

[1. FICTION / Short Stories (single author), 2. FICTION / Folklore,
3. FICTION / Small Town & Rural, 4. FICTION / Biographical,
5. FICTION / Literary, 6. FICTION / Historical 7. TRAVEL / Europe / Cyprus]

Translated from the Greek by *Despina Pirketti*

English text edited by *Lisa Suhair Majaj*

Cover: *Sea view of Famagusta with Glossa beach* (Mason01 | istockphoto)

~•~

Many thanks to the
Ministry of Education and Culture of the Republic of Cyprus
for financially supporting the translation of this work.
~•~

First published in Greek by *Iolkos* (Athens) in 2015 as *Ιστορίες της Αμμοχώστου*

1st English edition: February 2020

ISBN-13 (paperback): 978-9925-573-19-6

Dimitris Leventis

Stories of *Famagusta*

Translated by Despina Pirketti

Edited by Lisa Suhair Majaj

To my grandsons,
Dimitri and Stefano,
and to all the youth
of Famagusta:
to let them know

Memory that burns without burning
Affliction that won't simmer down.
Theodosis Nikolaou

Table of Contents

Daphne

Daphne thought that on that particular day she should light a candle to St Catherine at the small, rock-carved chapel on Demophon Street. It was at the root of Toumba, right at the beginning of the vertical road that leads to Kato Varosi; just five minutes away from her house. She had always relished walking into that sacred space where the scent of staleness and humidity was mixed with the smoke of the burning candles. She climbed up the rock, bowed her head to step in – in truth, Daphne's body was always bent – and walked down the steps until she reached the small landing with the icons. She lit her candle, bowed to kiss the icons, stood for a moment to supplicate in silence, and then crossed herself thrice. She always went to St Catherine to request the well-being of those dear to her. This time she asked for the safe, uneventful arrival of her sister, Maria, her brother-in-law, Pavlos, and their two-month old baby, Diomedes. They were travelling from Athens, where Pavlos was studying. On Sunday she had instructed the priest of St Nicholas, her parish, to make supplication. But today, when the ship was expected, she had to entreat the mediation of St Catherine herself.

As she made to step out, she heard a crawling sound and stopped. Thankfully, it wasn't a viper. A large lizard was scuttling rapidly through the dried high mallows.

The scene outside the cave spoke to her soul: the landscape, filled with wild flowers in full bloom in wintertime, dry and frequented by lizards and ants in summer, seemed to emit an earthly, unassuming, yet divine air of creation mingled with an age-old whisper of Christian adulation.

"They've ruined the place. They've trampled over the sacredness of the rock," Daphne would say later on, when a large church dedicated to St Catherine was erected on the flat expanse above the rock.

In the afternoon she went to the port with other relatives. Her elder sister, Eleni, was among them. On that particular day, the ship would not moor in Larnaka or Lemesos, but in Famagusta. While they waited for the ship to arrive, they walked along the large wooden dock where small boats were tied up to either side. They came back and walked along the waterfront, up and down, looking at the big vessels—mostly cargo ships—tied safely, almost touching, to the platform. They also cast their eyes on the walls that enclosed the west side of the port of Famagusta. The walls ran as far as Othello's Tower, which defined the port on its northern side. The walls had been there, almost intact, surrounding the old city since the 16th century, when they were rebuilt by the Venetians.

They saw the ship approaching from the south, but they didn't rush. They knew it would not enter the port immediately, for it had to move further north to bypass the islets and the reefs that hindered direct access and guarded the port against the tempest. "Desdemona," the launch, set out to meet the ship and guide it safely to the port.

"They're there!" Daphne exclaimed when the ship entered the port; "There, in the middle, at the lower part."

"How do you know it's them?" Eleni asked.

"They're waving handkerchiefs in a circle. This is what Maria usually does to stand out."

The ship berthed, the passengers disembarked, and everyone's eyes were cast on Diomedes. He was fair-skinned and blond. He looked like his father.

Daphne and Eleni didn't go to the house with the others straightaway. They passed through the gate that joined the port to the old city, and made toward the church of St George 'Exorinos' to light a candle in gratitude. That was the church Eleni went to regularly, her parish church. She lived in the area of the orange orchards outside the walls. Ahmet's pastry shop was on their street. They went inside and bought delicious baklava made by Aishe, Ahmet's wife, who had been a friend of Eleni's since the time they were both apprenticed to the best seamstress in Varosi.

Back then Varosi, initially a suburb of the old city, was a small town where the Greeks had taken residence after the city fell to the Turks in 1571, as they were shorn of the right to reside in the city within-the-walls. After Cyprus was ceded to England in 1878, the ban had been lifted. As it expanded, Varosi came to embrace the old quarter, and eventually the entire city was named Famagusta.

Aishe took it upon herself to send one of the carriages waiting outside the pastry shop— carriages were equivalent to taxis back then—to pick them up from the church after twenty minutes or so.

Eleni stood for a moment to look at the almond shrub in front of the house, a part of which had been turned into the pastry shop. The other two women, as though in cahoots, began declaiming the familiar tongue-tying phrase: "Aishe's shrubbiest shrubs sharply share their shapeless almonds." And they burst out laughing. Rarely did they laugh out loud. When she was little, enthralled by the tongue-tying phrase the girls at the seamstress used to playfully address to her, she had asked her father to plant her an almond shrub. Others say that the tongue-tying phrase came about precisely because Aishe already had an almond shrub in her yard.

They saw Ali coming out of the church with his wife. They were the couple that sold nuts in the central square. "That's odd," Eleni said, "coming here today, when there's no liturgy. Sometimes they attend Sunday mass."

The two women lit a candle and quickly boarded the carriage to exit the walls, passing through the main gate of the old city. After crossing the bridge over the moat, they proceeded past the hospital, the police station, and the District Administration Office, and reached the Jubilee, a small park made by the British on the fiftieth anniversary of Cyprus' occupation. There they stepped down from the carriage to walk a bit.

Daphne's house was very near. They lived close to the Frankish Church, the church of the Catholics, which Daphne had never entered, not even out of curiosity: so faithful was she to Orthodoxy.

"I'll be bringing Diomedes here to play," Daphne said, watching the children having fun on the swings and the other playground equipment in the Jubilee.

"We'll be taking photos too," she added, as she glanced at the open-air photographers with their tripods.

Daphne loved children and the entire world. She was a faithful Christian. Never married, she served her parents. Nobody ever asked if she had ever had her heart broken.

Within a few months, Cyprus was in the throes of the great war. Varosi was largely evacuated. Even the High School had been moved to Trikomo. But the people who lived in self-owned houses inside their orange orchards stayed put. Eleni was one of them. Daphne, Maria with the young Diomedes, and their parents found refuge in her orange orchard. At night they slept in the large storehouse near the reservoir with the windmill.

Daphne was not without her share of small sins. No sooner would she perceive the scent of fried potatoes coming from Eleni's kitchen, carried by the eastern wind that usually blew until noon, than she would walk out holding Diomedes in her arms.

Where are you off to again with the baby?" Maria would ask Daphne.

"We're just going for a stroll during his favourite time of the day," Daphne would reply.

Approaching Eleni's house, the boy would start yelling "tato," "tato." And it was a sin to indulge him because Daphne would then disobey Maria's instructions, and her principles to raise the baby on books and not on fried potatoes. Maria was one of the fine few graduates of the Girls' School, at that time the model Secondary Education Institution for girls.

They didn't stay for long at Eleni's. Maria, with Diomedes, went to Pavlos' village until her husband returned. Daphne and her parents moved to a different village where another of her sisters had sought refuge.

After the Allies' victory, Daphne and her parents went back to their own house, which would go on to become a meeting place for the wider family, especially during the summers, when the veranda with the blossoms offered an ideal setting for a chit-chat even with the people passing by on the street. The veranda was always crowded. Only her brother's motorcycle, parked in the corner with a small tray underneath to collect the dripping oil, was in the way. His daughter, Myrto, was a regular at the house, often buying 'koupes' meat pies from Ibrahim, a vendor who regularly passed by. She could hear him as he approached, announcing his presence by shouting "I have koupeeesss!" So much did she like them that she asked to know how to make and fry them. Hers were never as delicious as Ibrahim's, however, and she would blame it either on the bulgur, the onion, the minced meat, or the oil.

Myrto used to sit on the veranda with her grandfather, grandmother, uncles, aunts, and any cousins that happened to be there, waiting for her father to get off work so that they could ride back home together to their orange orchard in Laxis, two miles away. This did not happen very often, however, as Myrto usually rode her bicycle to come and go. That veranda and the house in general was dubbed "the Association" by the girls, the young cousins.

The young boys did not spend time in the Association. They would rather play hide-and-seek in the forest or football in the empty plot across the street with Aram and Dikran, their Armenian friends and neighbours. When playing hide-and-seek, they would spell out "embedi edei, embedi ok...," pointing to one boy at a time so that by the time the "chant" had finished, the seeker would be designated. Nobody knew the meaning of these words.

When darkness fell for good, the boys would return home with scraped knees and ankles for Daphne to tend to. Injured though they were, they would still tease Myrto on a whim over her fear of the worms in the low grapevine that roofed the veranda. The girl would only sit under sparse vines after thoroughly inspecting them first. Once the eldest cousin, an accomplished prankster, gave her an impressive matchbox for her collection. As soon as she opened it, Myrto let out a cry and threw it away. Inside a thick green worm, curled up, barely fit in the box.

When, in 1974, the Turks advanced to Famagusta, Daphne, like everybody else, abandoned her home. By then she had been left alone. Her parents had died after several years of being unable to care for themselves. Daphne had looked after them without so much as a complaint, as though this was precisely why she had never married.

For a few weeks she took refuge in a classroom

of an elementary school in Larnaka with ten other women; later on, in an abandoned Turkish house with another four. Then the state gave her a small house in the refugee housing of Tsiakkilero, with a small yard at both the front and back where she planted vegetables, jasmine, and a few geraniums. When she was no longer able to do her chores, her relatives put her in the Catholic Nuns senior home. It took the intervention of several relatives, especially her nephew, Diomedes, to convince her to dwell in a Catholic senior home. In the end she would even attend the Catholic mass. "They too are good Christians," she would say.

She left in peace and was buried in the Larnaka cemetery. Her grave stands out on account of the bay tree, in Greek known as 'daphne,' that Diomedes planted by the edge; so much has it grown! There is no other bay shrub nearby. Girls from the Lyceum across the street regularly cut branches from it to weave the wreaths that the school lays at the memorial services of the heroes.

It is rumoured that Daphne's 'daphne' branches are of special value – at least that's what a girl told the keeper at the cemetery when he chased after them as they cut the branches of the bay shrub. This girl also told him that her grandmother used to live next door to Daphne in Famagusta and that they had named her "Saint Daphne." He has not chased after them since.

The Shelter

The shelter was dug at the edge of Nitsa's orchard, by the long Salamis avenue that led from Famagusta to Salamis and beyond, to northern Mesaria and Karpasia. Her father had dug it quite far from their house, near the northern fence of the orchard, when, during World War II, the Italians bombed the port. Each time the sirens sounded, they all ran to the shelter.

They could find their way to the shelter even in pitch darkness, following the trail that led directly to it. The trail easily stood out because of the whitewashed stones that demarcated its two sides.

One night, awakened by the warning sirens, they rushed to the shelter. The sound of the sirens was followed by explosions of the bombs that the Italian airplanes dropped to strike the port. Shortly afterwards, a different sound was heard, as if something had crashed down not far from their orchard. When the airplanes left, they went looking; they found their neighbours from the orchard across from their own studying a bomb that had pierced the roof of their kitchen and lay there, still, instead of exploding. They were frightened, but not terrified. Would they always make mistakes, these Italians?

The war also brought an army of British and Indian men who on occasion camped in the large empty space outside the orchard. Little Nitsa would go over to check the comings and goings and they would give her biscuits and chocolates. Each time they left, her brother Mikis, a few years her elder, would casually stroll down the area in search of chocolates and biscuits that the soldiers had discarded in order to free up space in their kit bags and make them lighter.

From the same port, after the end of the war, other strangers came. These were the Jews that Britain had temporarily shipped to Cyprus on the way to their final destination, Palestine. The residents of Famagusta were helpful to those wretched human beings that had escaped the Germans' persecution. On occasion, Nitsa and her friends rode their bicycles just outside the camp in the Karaolos area near the sea. Her father and brothers were among the first to offer help. The Jews didn't stay long. The British took them to Palestine.

Salamis Avenue was flanked by orchards with the owners' houses located in them. Nitsa and Mikis played ball, backgammon, and card games with children from their neighbourhood.

At noon, the whole family gathered for lunch in the big dining room at the back of the house. Paschalis, Nitsa's father, used to tell stories from his life, from the time when he was a building contractor. He had also been a sculptor, having crafted capitals for churches and theatres. He had also crafted four small, ornate Corinthian columns for his four children. Yiannis, ever studious, would read the newspaper while eating.

Chores in the orchard were everyone's duty, but mostly Mikis'. Aside from the orange trees, he also tended to the countless beehives with bees flying about buzzing. To keep from being stung he wore gloves and a mask, which was more like a hat with tulle affixed around it, covering his face and neck. When he would open the beehives to either put the honeycombs in or take them out, he would use a special smoker to blow smoke at the bees. If the honeycombs were replete with honey, he got them out, took them to the honey lab, used a big sharp knife to remove the waxy cover the bees had lain over them to protect their harvest, and placed them into the cylinder of the honey extractor which, by spinning, flung the honey out of the honeycombs and into the cylinder. Last, he filled the jars that were arranged on the shelves of the laboratory. There they would note down the production of each hive for future reference. The one hundred and four hives were numbered, and the jars had coloured labels on them, printed abroad, picturing the blossom of an orange tree, if the honey was of spring production; or a branch of summer savory if it was of summer production from the mountains of Kantara where all the hives were transferred each summer. Spring honey was light-coloured with a faint scent.

To the left and right of the large corridor that led from the street to the house, fragrant white-yellow lilies blossomed in the spring, colourful zinnias in the summer. From there entered the cars that carried the oranges. The corridor was roofed by pergolas with grapevines, loaded with marvelous crunchy verigo grapes and sweet sultanas. On one side, outside the house, there was a small reservoir with fish, most of them red, and next to it two large swings where children and adults often played carefree. On the veranda there was a bee-hive made of glass that allowed you to observe the process followed by the bees. It was Yiannis who had made the hive, for he liked to watch the bees and keep track of their activities. He even published articles in a foreign specialized magazine he had subscribed to, which eventually secured him a scholarship. He liked to set up birdlimes around the hives in order to catch the bee-eaters, which were more than eager to devour his bees. Truth be told, the entire family was also more than eager to devour the caught bee-eaters.

Nitsa, a high school student, dedicated quite a lot of time to painting with oil on small wooden surfaces. Pantelis and Yiannis worked for trading companies. They all rode their bikes wherever they needed to go. Their father owned a three-wheeled bicycle which he rode to the city on Sundays with his wife and one or two of their children. Later on they bought a small car, a black Morris.

Nitsa rode to school and back with other girls from the area. She set out first, as her family's orchard was the farthest, crossed to the orchard across the street, and rang her bike bell to notify her friend to join her with her own bike. In this way, a large group of friends on bicycles gathered to ride together to the high school two miles away. They would pass by the main gate of the walls, sometimes stopping for a bit opposite the gate to drink water from the public tap.

In summertime they often rode to the sea. They would stop by their cousins' orchard across the street. Their uncle was a potter. With clay on the wheel he made large jars with ears, designed to keep the water cool during the summer; he made other pots too, which he fired in the large kiln. They would stop, chitchat with him and observe for a while the making of the pots. Then they would go on their way. Once they reached the rocks they descended very carefully in order to reach the sandy beach in Trypa. Other times they climbed up the wall from a half-ruined point, walked into the old city, and passed through the low arched Trypa gate to reach its sandy beach. The Trypa gate, supposed to be unknown to Medieval enemies, was on the eastern side of the walls that stretched to the north of the port. Sometimes, after swimming, they would stroll into the old city. That sandy beach no longer exists. It has been buried under the cement from the new port's platform.

Now and then, on their way back from the pottery, the uncle would give one of the littler ones a clay piggy bank, when he had learned from his daughter which boy or girl had broken their piggy bank: they usually did this on a feast-day, to buy something important.

When the EOKA liberating struggle was launched, Nitsa's family made the orchard and the house available for hiding ammunition in safe places dug under the orange trees, and for taking in and tending to wounded fighters who, in case of danger, crept into the old shelter which by then had been renovated. Nitsa too joined the Organization, but only for the activities that took place within the orchard, so as to be utterly beyond suspicion.

If, when the doctor was called in to tend to a wounded fighter, the family had guests, her mother, Xenia, feigned illness. This way, the doctor would retire to the bedroom with Xenia, supposedly to give her an injection, and Xenia would stay there for as long as the doctor needed to tend to the fighter's wounds.

Liberation from the British was achieved and life went on in the orchard without big changes. The children were married off and Paschalis and Xenia were left on their own.

Three years later, the Turks organized riots and created enclaves inhabited by Turks in the old city and in the area that was almost adjacent to the orchard. Their houses were built on plots they systematically bought from Greek land developers. Contacts with the old city ceased, as well as friendly relations with the Turks. But the orchard went on living.

A few weeks after the invasion of Cyprus, the Turkish army advanced towards Famagusta. The orchard was abandoned. The residents of Famagusta fled in terror of what they had heard or read about the atrocities in Kyrenia and elsewhere. The entire city was conquered by the Turks. Not a single soul remained there. The largest part of the new city, the core of Varosi, was fenced off and no one other than military was allowed to enter it.

Thirty years later, when the roadblocks were opened, Nitsa and her elder brother, Pantelis, went to visit their orchard that lay outside the fenced off area. The first time they passed by, they failed to recognize it. Salamis Avenue was beyond recognition. Construction, blocks of flats everywhere; the orchards had almost vanished. They turned back to see that their orchard too had been built over, at least along the side of the avenue.

They stopped for a while, then walked on, noticing there weren't many buildings further down the orchard. Some orange trees were still alive, as well as a palm tree near the reservoir. They left in silence.

At some point, while inside the car, Pantelis remembered.

"I wonder if they have discovered the shelter."

"Why?" Nitsa inquired, looking at him with curiosity.

"You never know! We might need it to chase them off."

The Cart Maker

When he ended up in Larnaka, a refugee from Famagusta, mastre Christodoulos could no longer get himself a proper job. Nor did he want to just sit idle and be counted as unemployed. Several years back he used to make carts. He was known as "Christodoulos the cart maker." When, around 1954, the number of autocars increased and carts were by law prohibited in the cities – gradually, in the villages too – he had set up a woodworking shop, his only trade when the making and repair of carts came to a halt. But he was still "Christodoulos the cart maker" to everyone. In Larnaka he found it impossible to reopen his woodworking shop. Money was scarce and by then he was quite elderly. To keep from sitting idly, he decided to make small carts for sale. Friends and relatives would buy them, to use as ornaments or as tokens of remembrance in their living rooms.

The first goal he had set himself was to make at least twenty small carts, though not of every kind. He had opted to make oxen-driven carts, specifically used for carrying agricultural products. These were his favourite carts because they had a peaceful power about them, a grandeur akin to that of the oxen. The miniature carts he made now measured 48 centimetres in length and 14 centimetres in wheel diameter: ten times smaller than actual carts. They were faithful replicas of real carts, and he sold them for twenty pounds apiece.

People said that when he was twenty years old his father, to whom he was apprenticed, had promised to transfer the family business to him on the day they would complete their twentieth cart together – an oxen-driven cart no less. Several years later, although customer orders didn't come about as often, his father indeed transferred the business to him.

He liked to work but he also liked to enjoy and relish life, always within the appropriate limits. He also liked to joke and play tricks on people. He was a prankster. He laughed even when he brought to mind the slap his father had given him, on the verge of entering adulthood, for coming home late one night to find the old man pacing in the large sunroom, his 'vraka' breeches billowing and his boots squeaking and landing hard on the big white gypsum tiles.

Mastre Christodoulos was happy making carts, but he was also happy with the wood business he had set up. Wooden planks leaned carefully against the walls of the large storehouse, arranged by type and height. On one side there were the hard yellowish Swedish woods, on the other side the soft white Romanian timber, with the wood-carving machine and the planer in the middle. He worked alongside his assistants, his hair and clothes sprinkled with sawdust and wood shavings. He had to be careful not to have a finger severed by the wood-carving machine, as had befallen one of his assistants.

In a corner he arranged a workshop for his father, mastre Kyriakos, who was reluctant to give up his trade altogether. Adzes, rasps, hammers, saws, and other tools were arranged in line. Every single tool was required in all different sizes. Aside from crafting the accessories of the carts, mastre Kyriakos also made helves for hoes, mattocks, and other tools; in fact, so skillfully would he apply them that they never fell. He was particularly good at making chairs. He assembled each piece not with glue or bolts, but by estimating the drilling of holes, estimating the required scraping, and securing the pieces with wedges. For special clients he would craft decorative lines, small circles and rosettes like the artisans of old used to do with fine furniture. At the end he would weave vegetable cord for the seat. This way, the chair was softer and cooler than those with plank seats, though on occasion it came to pass that bugs took residence within the cords.

For the helves he worked mostly with the Cypriot 'latzia,' the golden oak, and with Cypriot holm-oak which he himself bought during the summer, when he would spend twenty days on the Troodos mountains in his favourite village of Askas, buying supplies. He toured villages and mountains to find the appropriate type of wood. He would go as far as 'Kambos of Tsakistra' if he could find a ride. He didn't live long enough to see the 'latzia' being proclaimed Cyprus' national tree.

The holm-oak he needed for another reason too. When mothers with sick babies brought him a red thread measuring the height of the baby, he would unroll the thread along a thick branch of holm-oak and cut thin slices with the large adze, all the while muttering the proper prayers. The mothers took the wood slices home and set them on fire to heat water for the baby's bath. Some of them, if the water was too harsh, would burn the slices to ashes which they then added to the water jar to make 'alousiva,' a kind of soap which they then used to bathe the babies with. Some babies wouldn't get better, and then the mothers would complain he didn't say all the prayers or that he didn't cut the holm-oak properly. This was a special skill that was passed down to mastre Christodoulos.

Mastre Kyriakos, being a commissioner at St Nicholas church, was also interested in Christian education. In fact, on occasion he would copy out religious articles from the "Sion" magazine and send them to the Religious Association of Askas for his friends to read, as the Association could not afford a subscription to the "Sion."

From Askas he usually brought a demijohn of sweet red wine. When the demijohn ran out, every three or four days, he would send his grandson with an empty bottle to the nearby wine station of Hadjipavlos to have it refilled from the wine barrel. This grandson, a first grader in high school, would sit across from him at the table. "Woman," the grandfather would exclaim, "bring the boy a glass to keep me company." The boy lived with his grandparents, seeing that there was no high school in the village where his parents lived.

Going through life as a refugee, mastre Christodoulos always remembered his father with respect. And now, as though the old man would observe and grade him from above, he made sure the small carts were crafted as thoroughly as ever. The planks had to fit without glue or nails or bolts. Of course, the axle, the roller bearings, the rims, and very few other parts were made of metal. He would go from one Larnaka artisan to another, those he used to associate with when he lived in Famagusta, before the Turkish invasion and the city's occupation, and they would willingly supply him with the appropriate wood and metal.

Nor did he make any exception in his technique for the 'kaplamades,' the iron rims of the two wheels which were heated and placed, expanded, on the wooden wheels. Back then, they would place the wooden spoked wheel, its diameter slightly greater than the internal diameter of the iron rim, in the open field across from the workshop and the woodworking business. A bit beyond the wheel, the iron rim would be laid over several pieces of wood. When they were ready, the men would light the wood up with petroleum. The whole place would be covered in smoke. When the iron was red, the rim expanded. At least four robust craftsmen would grab it with huge pincers on the "go" and fit it quickly around the wooden wheel. The wood would smoke and creak as the men hammered the incandescent iron with their bats to forge it. There was no room for mistakes. Within very little time they had to finish, and then pour plenty of water over the iron to cause it to contract, to settle tightly on the wood and stay there solidly for as long as the cart would last. Once again, there was steam, creaking and yelling, panting and sweating. Then they would sit down and marvel. And they would drink water, lots of water.

The only exception he made was regarding the colour. The customers didn't want their carts dyed blue and white, like the real carts in circulation during British rule in Cyprus, reminiscent of the Greek flag. They wanted them varnished; so, against his deeper wishes he had to varnish them with that soulless glazing polish. "Who had ever heard of varnished carts!" he used to fret. "Along with the cause of *Enosis* to Greece, so too the Greek colour was lost," he would add. In the sitting room the carts looked better varnished, his customers would retort.

Of course, they did appreciate the fact that the wheels turned smoothly. If they gave them a firm push, they would go on turning for quite some time. And mastre Christodoulos would look at his customers with a winning smile on his face and an inquiring, triumphant look in his eyes, rightfully anticipating their words of admiration. But for everything else, all the details, they had no idea. He didn't mind. He explained everything himself, and he enjoyed it too.

He told them that the wheels with the iron rims had been abolished with the advent of rubber wheels. And when the number of trucks increased, the carts were completely gone. "We loved them," he would say, "because they were made with the same wood we hewed with our sweat. And they ran at a slow pace. You could hear them from afar." He would also tell them about the registration number of each cart, listed in the official records. On the cart itself, the number was inscribed on a small metal plaque and bolted high up, to be visible to the competent authorities. The small carts he made for decoration had a serial number he would give them based on his own records, where he would note down the name of the customer, and the starting date and delivery date for each cart.

The twentieth cart he made for Elias, an old customer of his from a village in Mesaoria. Elias was close to a hundred years old. "Truly, you are still the best master," he told him when he received the cart. "You forgot nothing, changed nothing. You've placed a big yoke beam to easily accommodate the oxen to the left and to the right, and the drawbar on the edge. Each time I finished tying the harness with the bunch of straps on the drawbar, and fitted the harness with the warped sticks on the neck of the oxen, I mounted that cart with so much pride."

"Pride in what?" mastre Christodoulos asked.

Not heeding the question, Elias went on. "The side sticks you've also arranged nicely, fastened vertically onto the bed without glue and bolts, just like back then. And also, the curved elbows on the front and back, to support the sides of the cart." He stopped talking and kept on looking.

At that moment, Christodoulos' little grandson walked in. "Come learn about carts from a great farmer of the days of yore," he told the boy, who was fond of listening to old stories. Then he turned to Elias: "You didn't mention the swivel in the rear of the bed. Don't you think it's good?" Mastre Christodoulos spoke strongly, because he thought very highly of the function of the wooden rotating cylinder with the projecting nail and the two holes pierced through the cylinder at a vertical distance from each other.

"Hold your horses!" Elias said. He went on to re-live unforgettable moments from his life, happily talking to a man who understood him and proudly elaborating for the sake of the child. "After loading the sheaves, I would take great pleasure in unfolding the rope; one edge was tied back, this is how I preferred it, and the other edge I would cast over the sheaves on the front part of the bed. I would pass it through the big ring that was bolted to the right, on the edge of the bed, like you did now, and then through the left ring. I would throw the rope back, pass it through the cylinder which, from what I can see, you've also crafted to perfection, and tie it to the nail. I would place an iron tightener in one hole and stretch the rope by rotating the cylinder for half a round, and then another tightener into the other hole, another half round, once with one hole and once with the other, until the rope would tighten up and hold the sheaves safely in place. I remember how much strength I needed to apply to tighten up the rope. And then, dripping sweat, I would set out on my way back." He stopped again and looked at the cart with piercing, yet loving, eyes. The two men kept silent for quite some time.

"Please allow me to add a couple of fittings to it," Elias said. "On the projections of the side boards I want to hang a small clay jug and a tiny woven basket. I will make them myself, to remind me of the time when I used to stop under the scorching sun to drink water and eat something in the shade of the cart when there was no tree near. Also, to water the oxen, and give water to my dog, Pohouzouris, who liked to stroll under the cart. The biggest heat came when we would mow the wheat. You do know that wheat ripens slower than barley." The grandson relished the story. "Bravo, grandpa," he said, and went over to the workbench to carry on making a small house.

They went on talking long and nostalgically about the peaceful old times; when people didn't run everywhere nor did carts – all carts, not just the oxen-driven ones. Even the lightly loaded carts drawn by a horse or a mule didn't travel fast. They would roll faster but calmly, with the horse between the long helms, as they called the beams projecting from the base of the bed.

From the day he completed his twentieth cart, his last one, he kept to himself in his small house. He lived there alone, behind his daughter's house. His wife had died several years before. Now the site of her grave was occupied by the Turks, and he couldn't visit to lay a few flowers there and talk to her about their children's achievements. But they could still hear him rasp, saw, grind. When they asked, he said he was just passing time without looking to make something in particular.

Then from one day onwards, silence reigned. Mastre Christodoulos looked happy even without working. He died a few months later. His daughter found him sitting in his bed when she went to offer him a slice from the cake she had just baked. He liked cakes very much. A faint smile illuminated his face, his gaze cast on the table across from him. Placed on the table was a small blue-and-white cart; just like the flag. Without a number.

The Missing Man

"Aren't you wary of the Turk?" Flourentzos kept cautioning his cousin, Pieris. "He might steal your potatoes and then all our trouble will go to waste. Where did you find him anyway?" Flourentzos was worried that the Turk with the truck whom he had hired to drive the large baskets of potatoes to the storehouses of the Cooperative in Famagusta would not keep his end of the bargain, and would instead sell them for his own profit in the walled city. Ever since the Turks had barricaded themselves there, it wasn't easy to drive into the area and stand up for your rights; in fact, to do so would be dangerous.

All day they had been harvesting potatoes from Pieris' large plot of land. As many as fifteen relatives were toiling there. This is what they always did, moving in swarms from one plot to another. By the end of the day they would all be completely red. Hands, shoes, shirts, trousers, hats, flushed faces. The red soil of Kokkinochoria is the best for potatoes, as it is for so many other things, so it's well worth it, reddening up everything. It's the best soil for every potato variety: Arran Banner, Up-to-Date, Spunta. They say that Spunta is best cooked in the oven. And red soil is so good for them that in nearby villages the white-grey soil of entire fields had been removed and replaced with red, brought there from the nearby Red-Soil villages, the 'Kokkinochoria.'

Pieris took Flourentzos aside and explained. "I knew nothing of him. A Turkish man I knew spoke well of him; he said he's the son of Bayazit, the old policeman, a man of fine repute. And then an old story came to mind."

"How old do you mean?"

"Now we're in 1971. The story transpired in 1957, which means fourteen years ago. Let's go to my place for coffee, I'll tell you all about it."

They each mounted their tractors, the others following on their bikes, and set out for the village. With them was Selim, invited not only for coffee but also for dinner. He knew what was on the main menu. Lamb on a spit, beccaficos, cypress tree mushrooms—some were kept in the freezer at all times—and leaves of coriander and rocket. Selim relished cypress tree mushrooms, a rarity, fried with eggs. The first time he was invited, he didn't know he would join them for dinner, so he brought nothing with him. After that, each time they asked him to dinner he brought a tray of baklava.

They ate, had coffee, rested, Selim left, and then came the time for the story.

"Before I took the decision to cultivate potatoes,

I used to work at an office in Famagusta," Pieris began. "I had just graduated from high school. That I was detained by the British you do know, but you don't know the details. I had become a member of the EOKA along with others from our village. You were very young at the time. I used to live in Famagusta. Eventually I joined this group that threw hand grenades against British military buildings and cars. But that's a different story."

"Well?"

"One morning, as I was working at the office, policemen stepped in and asked for our IDs. I noticed that the man who was collecting the IDs held mine between different fingers. Right then I knew. They put me into the Land Rover where another man was waiting. We pretended not to know each other. They arrested an additional four and took us to the police station of the old city, where the interrogation rooms were, then threw us into the cells. I was in the same cell with an EOKA fighter who had been wanted for some time; they only got him after a fight. I knew him. He described how they had tortured him. My fear grew bigger; not for the pain but lest they would break me. I was sure they wouldn't, but the fear was always there."

"Did they torture you?" Flourentzos asked.

"Except for a slap, the interrogators didn't torture me. Officer Bayazit was there too. On hearing my unusual surname, he asked me whether I was the son of Paris. I nodded yes and he said, "Such a waste for Paris to have had such a son." Afterwards I wondered whether it was he who hadn't let them torture me, seeing how frail I was, out of appreciation for my father. They used to play backgammon together when Officer Bayazit was serving in our village. Anyhow, they had nothing solid against me. In the official records the cause for my arrest was specified as 'throwing hand grenades.' I never found out who had snitched on me.

"In the cell they brought us bread and herring. As for water, they only gave us one bottle. We had a second one to pee in. Mercifully, we didn't mix them up."

"Selim looks friendly enough," Flourentzos said. "I'll ask him to transport my own potatoes too, now that my brother-in-law has had an operation."

And so he did. Selim became their regular driver. Sometimes he was also invited to their homes for dinner. They didn't discuss the disputes between Greeks and Turks. Only one time did Selim wish to say something. "You are kind-hearted and you love people. Why don't you love us Turks too? We've lived in this land for so many years now." Silence reigned. It was only broken by Flourentzos, who said, "You don't let us love you." That was the last time they spoke of it.

In the meantime, the small orange orchard that Flourentzos had planted around his house had grown, and his children were happy to tend to it and enjoy the fruit it bore. Their grandfather, who lived next door and could no longer toil in the fields, had shared with his grandchildren all the secrets he knew.

Along one side, the orchard had fig trees and a prickly pear. Their grandfather had taught them how to nail an empty milk can onto a long rod and use it to harvest the prickly pear fruits, then put them into a metal bucket with cold water and rinse them to get rid of the needles on their skin. Then they would carefully make a vertical slit on either end and another one along the length of the fruit in order to peel the skin away and reach its tasty content—tasty indeed, though the seeds took away from its worth. But the purple figs were marvelous. On the other end of the orchard, there was a lemon tree, two olive trees, and two pomegranates. Their grandfather had taught them how to distinguish between the pomegranate's male and female flowers. Only the female flowers produced fruit; they checked them often, to see how they grew.

They also had a vegetable garden that provided them with tomatoes, cucumbers, okras, peppers, green butter beans, black-eyed beans, zucchini 'palkapa' – namely marrows – and much more. The old man was particularly fond of black-eyed beans boiled with zucchini, accompanied by a side dish of sardines or herring.

He would take long walks with them outside the orange orchard, sometimes to pick mushrooms or 'agrelia,' wild asparagus. Their grandmother would fry these with eggs at night. They were overjoyed each time they stumbled on a particular variety of small wild artichokes, just above the ground, which they would also fry with eggs.

All these plants, as well as the adjacent large potato field, were watered from the windmill. As it turned, the mill fed water into a tank and from there, with the ditches at the right gradient to allow water to flow, it was channeled into the basins and the small furrows. Their grandfather had taught them how to rearrange the soil with the hoe and channel the water into each basin or small trench.

The old man was also on good terms with the teacher from Nicosia, until one day the teacher told him that, judging from the family's blond-haired members, and considering their peculiar names, they were probably descended from the Francs. And not just them, but most of the Kokkinochoria residents. He never forgave him for that.

The quiet, laborious life at home and in the village was abruptly, awfully interrupted by the invasion of the Turks. Pieris and Flourentzos enlisted immediately and were deployed to the front lines.

When a truce was finally reached, Pieris returned home. They were trying to locate Flourentzos, asking those who might had seen him. They found out he had made it up to Marathovounos. Nowhere else had he been seen.

A few weeks after the end of the war, Selim sent a man to the British Base at Tessera Mili, which Greeks and Turks alike had access to and where they worked, to ask an acquaintance of his from Kokkinochoria for news of Pieris and Flourentzos. On hearing that one of them was missing, he asked for the other one to meet him at the Base and help him get news of the missing man's whereabouts.

Pieris went to the Base. Selim himself was there to welcome him. On the way to the old city, Pieris was scared for his own life. He had lost his trust. The Turks knew Selim and so they were waved through the checkpoint. It was obvious that he was of a fairly high rank, and that in the previous years he had taken his driver's job for spying. Once in the old city, they went to the Central Services and searched through several lists and photographs, but came up with nothing. That was the last time Pieris saw Selim.

Flourentzos' wife never believed her husband would come back. She dressed in black for mourning and decided that this is where her life as she knew it would end. From that day on, she became the wife of the missing man, her children the children of the missing man.

Forty years later, Flourentzos is still missing.

They never found his bones for a proper burial. As for his wife, after her children got married, every night when she closed her door and took off her black robes, she only thought of Flourentzos and their village.

For her and their children, Flourentzos was always there, strolling among the trees in the courtyard, watering the plants and laughing and singing. And he lived on in the heart of little Flourentzos, who had heard so many stories about his grandfather. But the boy was never really without a grandfather. His family and the small society of the village had plenty of grandfathers; good grandfathers, too.

The Tavern

"See these four guys that just stepped in? Want to know what they ordered? A small V.O. with its meze! And they were smiling, too," Grigoris the waiter told the tavern owner for a second time, as the latter looked on with a condescending smile.

Taverns had removed this option from their menus, that's why Grigoris was puzzled. He had grown old in the trade and of late he forgot faces and things. Besides, he had been away in Canada for some forty years before deciding to end his days in his homeland, with his old boss, no less. It was only a few days since he had started working for him again.

"Have you forgotten all about the old customers from Varosi?" Liasis asked him. Liasis used to own a small tavern in Varosi. For years a refugee, now he had managed to set up his own tavern in Limassol. Then he added: "It's Thomas, isn't it? With his usual crew."

"By God, you're right! But they've gone grey! I haven't seen them since the late sixties. Boss, do you remember back then when we were liberated from the Brits, and they would come in a group of eight, drinking and singing patriotic songs?

And how the other customers stared at them with open curiosity?"

Liasis was thoughtful for a while and then he said: "I remember. These men, while the struggle was still on, were either wanted, detained, or imprisoned. The homeland was their sweetheart. Don't they sing about their sweethearts in the tavern – whether faithful or unfaithful?"

"You only just avoided the same fate, boss; it was a narrow escape. I remember the Brits storming into the tavern for a search, but they skipped the bathroom because one of them had to use it straight away. So they didn't find the pistol brought to you after each hit, the one you had tucked behind the toilet. Those were the times! Say," Grigoris inquired, his eyes cast on the men, "how did you recognize them?"

"I saw them a few times in Larnaka, when I visited my sister. But they were here again, some three or four years ago."

"Yes, it all comes back to me now. What ever happened to the other three?"

"It's a long story. Now, serve them a small bottle with its meze and see what they have to say. We'll return their joke! See, they placed this particular order to tease you, to trigger your memory, and you didn't get the joke. We've grown old, Grigoris!"

When he served them a bottle with twenty small dishes, the four of them, surprised at the recurrence of the old habit, chaffed Grigoris and set out sipping their cognac, sampling a bit of the meze as they drank. This way, they said, they wouldn't get drunk, and they would enjoy more drinks. They didn't always order V.O. When they were young, they settled for a one-star cognac, but they were told tough men had to drink V.O. or even V.S.O.P.

The time passed and the bottle was almost empty when Liasis called Grigoris to him and instructed: "Get them a second bottle with its dishes and tell them it's on the house. But first... They used to be eight, now they're four. Why did you ask me about the other three?"

"Because the fourth one I used to see in Canada. I didn't want to talk about him, but since you've brought it up, I'll tell you. You do know he was in EOKA B. After the coup, the invasion, and the disaster, he came to Canada because he felt betrayed and ashamed. Twice I saw him at the revolving restaurant on the high tower of the city of Niagara Falls, where I worked. He was in bad shape. One night, apparently, he couldn't take it anymore and... he fell to his death from the roof of the multi-storey building where he worked on the ground floor. Perhaps that's why he had made those comments about the construction of the revolving restaurant, that its windows were sealed, they wouldn't open. Last time I saw him, he talked a lot about his grave. He imagined it strewn with flowers. I just felt that his wish was for his body and soul to find peace in a cemetery. So, he didn't plunge over Niagara Falls and perish like so many others in the area. Obviously, you never heard," Grigoris said, and started preparing the tray with the second bottle.

"Get them some of the wine-sausages from Pitsilia too," Liasis discreetly told him. He took pride in the fact that he hailed from Palaichori, a main village in the mountainous region of Pitsilia. Oddly enough, many Palaichorians ended up in Famagusta instead of Nicosia, which was closer. They helped one another, just like Liasis did with Grigoris.

A bit later, Liasis grabbed a chair and a glass and joined his friends' table. After some small talk and chaffing about old age, he told them the news about the suicide. Thomas, welling up, remarked: "Why did they use EOKA's name? They shouldn't have done anything in the name of EOKA. It certainly attracted many. But it was a big mistake. Now they purposely confuse EOKA with EOKA B; even worse, they are considered the same. Thankfully we kept back. But they just won't separate us from them. It serves them and others better this way."

When all the other customers left, Grigoris sat with them too, and asked about the other three. "One of them made lots of money, the other one married some posh woman, and the third one is lost to us, he's into politics," Thomas replied. The four of them could not, or rather, would not change their fortunes, either financially or socially.

"I see," Grigoris said. "You insist on your own ways. Good friends, cognac, and a kind heart. It's for these things that I've returned to Cyprus. For as long as they shall be."

Liasis and Grigoris had two drinks with them, then withdrew.

The four hadn't been able to empty the second bottle. Back when they were young, they would probably have drunk up a third and a fourth one, to show they could hold their liquor without getting drunk.

Long they stayed there, talking, laughing, making conversation. Liasis' tavern in Limassol prompted one of many discussions on how the residents of Famagusta were scattered everywhere, not only across the free cities and villages of Cyprus but also of Greece, and the whole world even!

They would often talk about drinking habits. One of them, whose brother had found his way from Famagusta to Volos, said that along the coastline there, a succession of fish taverns served fish meze for every small 50 ml bottle of tsipouro.

The other one's brother settled in Kythera where there was a town named Karavas, just like in Kyrenia. In fact, Aphrodite is said to have been born both in Kythera and in Pafos. He relayed all this in a way that suggested Cyprus was everywhere, but more specifically to add that, when he visited his brother, he had to take a boat from Neapolis. He missed the boat, however, and so he spent the night there, sipping retsina with a group of friends, relishing grilled octopus. The entire coastal front was filled with outdoor grills cooking nothing but octopus. The scent of grilled octopus wafted in the streets until late, very late into the night.

"The fate of the pomegranate has befallen us, mates," one of them said.

"What's the pomegranate got to do with us?"

"We used to be assembled within our Varo-si, closely-knit and vibrant, like the seeds of the pomegranate, organized in chambers. And then the Turks beat down on us and broke us asunder; or rather, we banged our head against the Turkish wall within us and shattered."

"We're not young anymore, guys," one of them said. His phrase was out of context; and yet they all took it in.

They kept silent for some time; then they sang just one song, the "Sergeant."

These two verses they sang thrice and rose to their feet:

> *Look at us now, sergeant,*
> *Who am I, who are you!*

"Goodnight, Varosi," they told the tavern.

"Goodnight, Tepelene," the tavern owner declared.

None of them cared to specify whether they sang for their forgotten achievements from the time they were fighting in the name of Enosis, or for their old age.

The Coin

They used to hop on their bikes and ride around every afternoon across the entire city, Michalis and his group of friends, even as high school sophomore students. It was October 1954 when they passed outside the harbour. Hasan, Michalis' Turkish friend, was with them too. Michalis lived in the city-within-the-walls, near the Greek elementary school. They didn't feel like taking in the crowd at the harbour again, so they decided to pick the capers growing on the wall and in the moat. They all enjoyed pickled capers. The moat along the walls was usually deserted and the capers left untouched. Only a few young couples in love met there at night.

As they were picking capers, Michalis told them a story he had heard from his cousin Roula. As a little boy, an uncle of hers from her mother's side used to play with a friend of his in the streets and the area behind the police station, as well as around the walls on the opposite side, all these places being relatively close to their house. One day, after torrential rain, they discovered a small vessel scarcely visible in the earth, which upon investigation proved to be filled with golden coins. A police officer caught sight of them as they were digging the vessel out of the ground, reprimanded them, and took the vessel. These were ancient objects, he told them, and he had to deliver them to the police. There were several stories like that going around, mostly of smaller finds, but this one in particular had them looking for something else aside capers.

Michalis was lucky. In a crevice he found a black coin, its inscriptions and images completely shrouded. Not knowing how to handle a coin like this, he rubbed it against the ground. Its copper glowed and he made out the year, 1570, along with a figure of some sort with wings. He was elated. Later on, he would discover that he was only one among several others who had found similar coins.

Hasan found a different coin that was bigger and better preserved, with letters in old Turkish, namely in the Arabic script. They had both started collections of coins, stamps, matchboxes, and other items, so they knew how to read the numbers in Arabic. This coin had the number 20 inscribed on one side, along with the date 1277, while on the other side it pictured the "toughra," the Sultan's intricate signature. At high school, whenever they tossed a coin, even the Greeks exclaimed "ghazi-toughra." Later, "ghazi-toughra" came to be replaced by "heads or tails". Hasan claimed that they had to add 582 years to get to the equivalent Christian date. So, the coin was dated 1859. Even though Michalis had been taught in history class that Muslims counted time from 622 AD, the year of Muhammad's migration to Medina, and therefore they should add 622 years to arrive at the equivalent date, he refrained from mentioning this. Perhaps there were differences from one country to the other.

When Michalis went home he cleaned the coin more thoroughly. He had trouble making out the letters. Then he realized they looked like Latin. He had been taught Latin at school, so he used the dictionary. There was a circular inscription on the coin, "PRO REGNI CIPRI PRESIDIO," which he deciphered as "For the garrison of the kingdom of Cyprus." On the reverse side, it read "VENE-TORUM FIDES INVIOLABILIS," arranged in three lines. This translated as "The trustworthiness of the Venetians is inviolable." And at the bottom it read "BISANTE 1," which meant "One byzant". The byzant was the currency then circulating in the West, equivalent to the Byzantine "Constantinato" coin minted by Constantine the Great, which was preserved by succeeding emperors for some seven hundred years. Looking for more information, Michalis found that the coins had been struck both in Nicosia and in Famagusta to pay the wages of the soldiers, both Venetians and Greeks, who fought the Ottoman invaders in 1570 and, more generally, for the needs of the state. He also learned that bronze coins would be exchanged for authentic byzants. He wondered if after the fall of Famagusta in 1571 there had been some who, regardless of nationality, had survived the Turkish atrocities and fled to Venice to redeem their coins.

Michalis learned a lot from coins, stamps and matchboxes. He kept collecting coins until he graduated from the 10th grade. Then he became interested in other things.

When the Turks were advancing on Famagusta in the summer of 1974, Michalis prepared some luggage for his wife and children. He himself was on duty. Into the luggage he placed the coin collection; not because of its monetary value, but because he had put it together himself.

After they had become refugees, faced with so many needs, he went to a special shop in Nicosia to ask how much they would pay for his collection. Seeing that the displaced man was in dire need of money, the Nicosian shopkeeper proposed a humiliating price. So Michalis opted to keep the coins. He could just as well offer them to someone as a gift.

Much later, when the Ministry sent him to a conference in Venice, he remembered the coin he had discovered searching for capers that day with his friends. He thought he should take it with him and ask the city's authorities to exchange it with a golden byzant, in reciprocity for everything the

Christians had suffered to keep the Turks away from Europe. It was a casual thought, out of curiosity mostly, and, of course it would only matter if European Christians still wanted the Turks away from Europe.

In fact, when he attended the conference in Venice, which was addressed by the mayor of the city, Michalis suggested the idea and the mayor was thrilled. He even proposed organizing a special event to bring out the symbolism of the gesture. They had plenty of byzants, they didn't mind giving away one. After all, Venice and Larnaka had recently become twinned cities, with a Venetian lion recently installed on the coast of the latter. Michalis wondered who had taken that decision; the lion was near the bust of Cimon the Athenian, at that, who died there fighting for the freedom of Cyprus.

The mayor accompanied his guest to the museum where, among other exhibits, he could see the golden coin. There it was, glowing. Michalis took the bronze coin out of his pocket and looked at it; then he looked back at the golden one. He smiled to the mayor. "It's best that I keep this one," he said. With that, he put the bronze coin back into his pocket and left. As he walked out in the cold of winter, he dived into his pocket and clenched his fingers around the coin. He thought it warmed up his palm.

The Student Surveillant

"Buy yourselves a bag while you're at it," Takis the hunchback told the three eleventh graders of the Hellenic Gymnasium of Famagusta. Takis was a peddler; they called him hunchback to distinguish him from so many other men called Takis. The boys had parked their bicycles on the large terrace of the Hadjichambis movie theatre, and now stood under the small tent that Takis had put up over his cart. It drizzled every now and then that day, otherwise they would have left their bicycles by the stairs next to Takis' cart. It was cold too, even though spring had come and a scent of orange blossoms wafted over the entire city. They stood there with their hands near the funnel that poured out smoke from the charcoal. Takis kept an open fire to warm up the whole peanuts, covered with a layer of salt on the outside but delicious when you cracked them open and ate them; so fresh were they, of the latest crop. Every once in a while, they lowered their hands and grabbed a peanut to pass the time.

"We'll buy a bag when Theodoros gets here too, to eat while we walk. And you should add several drams for free, since you've put too much salt today." Takis said nothing. He only smiled. He didn't

mind the boys' jokes. They were regular customers during the summer too, when he rented them
boats for a ride. The boats were anchored off Glossa
beach and he instructed them how to drive them,
warning them not to stray far from the coast and,
most of all, not to bang them against the rocks.
He was more concerned about the canoes, as they
were easier to topple over if the boys maneuvered
them recklessly for fun. In a rough sea, when he
saw them press on to make the round of Kamila,
the farthest small rock, he would keep his eyes on
them until they paddled the canoes back.

People munched their peanuts as they strolled
up and down, throwing the shells on the ground.
After all, they had to give street cleaners something to do. Men and women alike walked back
and forth along the small route. Some of the
young girls were followed by their parents. It was a
demarcated route; from the pharmacy on the corner with Hermes Street, which was the commercial strip, down to a bit further than Ideal Cinema.
Late in the afternoon and early in the evening
the street took on a different name: it became the
Stroll. "I will see you at the Stroll," they used to
say. Only a handful of them knew that its actual
name was "King Edward XIII."

Theodoros joined them and he too reached out
his hand for a peanut, before buying a bag and
starting to stroll up and down.

"Ah! I forgot to tell you, the surveillant is inside the cinema, waiting to snatch any student that might dare to step in," Takis told them.

"And how do you know he hasn't left?"

"His bike is still there."

"But if he got out without you seeing him and he went to the Heraion, where Neophytos is now watching Logothetides, Neophytos is in big trouble."

"Now go take your stroll and don't mind the surveillant," Takis said in a bid to put an end to the peanut-snatching.

The friends walked leisurely, commenting on the surveillant, who was employed by the School Board to observe the behaviour of the students in and out of the school. They also commented on the schoolgirls who always walked separately. Not many people went as far as the next section of the street, where the cafeteria Phaliro was built on the sand of Glossa beach, or down to Aktaion, a bit further to the south. It was dark too, at night, therefore suitable only for young couples in love.

Sometimes, before taking the turn to the coastal cafeterias they would buy a newspaper cone of roasted hemp seeds. They knew the seeds, which were also canary food, were the fruits of the hemp plant. Many summer taverns would grow hemp plants for greenery. The boys also knew that hashish too was extracted from the hemp plant, and that some were addicted to it—the junkies, looked down upon by people. But the roasted seeds were sold legally and were a good alternative to peanuts.

At the photo studio, they paused to check whether they had been captured in any of the photographs taken the day before during the high school celebration at "Gasie," the stadium of the city's Evagoras Gymnastics Association. The photographs, numbered, were affixed to a blackboard-sized panel on a tripod.

They perused and they ordered.

"Write this one down, too," Theodoros said.

"But you're not in it," Sakis remarked. "Oh, for Chloe, right?"

"Yes, for Chloe, and I'll even put it in a frame!"

"You might as well, since you can't touch her!"

The next day, Theodoros suggested they walk as far as the sea. Once there, he told them goodbye, left, and walked to one of the sparse benches in front of the Aktaion, his feet resting on sand moistened by the sea swell. They watched him inquisitively until they saw Chloe overtaking them from the other side of the street, her eyes turned away. They soon realized she had walked ahead of the group of the other girls and was going straight to the bench. They weren't supposed to stay there. The boys turned back and saw the surveillant riding his bicycle straight to the beach. There was nothing they could do. One of them raised his hand to tell him something, but the surveillant merely greeted and went on. And of course, he caught the young couple.

That's how Theodoros paid for his determination to prove he could touch Chloe. The following day they were both suspended for ten days. The entire school, the whole city even, talked about the incident for days on end.

Either that suspension was fate or their love was great; or both. They never cared to probe deeper. They lived together to a ripe old age.

In any case, the surveillant, pleased with his unusual feat, declared that punishment for breaking the law does good and puts sense into a person.

The Avengers

The bicycle was more or less the only road vehicle back then, even for teachers. Students took bike rides in the afternoons through every street in Famagusta, courting girls from their school, who either sat on their verandas or stood by their windows. At some point, Demos and Andreas and their group of friends would have covered all the usual streets at the centre, and would park for a while at "Kypseli" for pastries.

One day they rode as far as the harbour, because a passenger ship would soon be arriving and they wanted to take in the crowd. Not many passenger ships sailed to Famagusta at the time; the harbour was Cyprus' main commercial harbor, as it was the only one where ships moored at the dock. They crossed Evagoras Avenue and, before making it to the harbour, passed by Brago's, which sold paraphernalia for seamen, swimmers, and fishermen. Tourhan was there too, Andreas' friend.

Tourhan lived in the old city. Andreas' home, with a small orange orchard, was located right outside the walls, almost adjacent to the moat that surrounded them. Andreas and Tourhan often played together at the moat, along the walls, and in the forest of the Turkish Lyceum, opposite the main gate out of the walls. Many times, Demos was with them too.

At Brago's they marveled at the spear guns and other equipment. They were intrigued by a big bronze antique compass, even though they knew they couldn't afford anything with the small allowance their parents gave them. Soon enough they would be able to, though, once they got jobs.

"Could he be Italian?" Andreas wondered out loud when they stepped outside.

"Perhaps he's the descendant of some Venetian who survived the conquest of Famagusta, either because he was in some village or because he showed up after the massacre, when the city surrendered to Lala Mustafa in August 1571," declared Demos, who had delved into the history of Cyprus.

"What massacre?" Tourhan retorted. "It's not enough we saved you from the Catholics and gave you a ton of privileges, now you accuse us? After all, this is how any war goes. And from what I have learned, Markantonio Bragadin, the leader of the Venetians, executed all the Turks he held captives even though he had promised to set them free upon the city's surrender."

"These are all lies they conjured to justify the massacre, like they always did, teeming with hatred over the losses they had suffered during twelve months of siege. Anyway, let's get to the harbour.

Are you coming, Tourhan?" Tourhan joined them, albeit sulking.

They entered the harbour. The eastern entrance was permanently open, just like the gate in the walls that led into the old city. The corner bastion and the entire wall, its external eastern side facing the harbour, was more or less well-preserved. The yellow-brown carved stones were still firmly stuck together, except at the points where caper bushes and other plants grew and hung, their roots causing erosion to the time-worn joints. Crowds of people strolled down the pier and the waterfront. They were waiting for their loved ones, either returning immigrants or students who had boarded the ship. There were but few tourists at the time. When the ship anchored, the ladder came down and the young cyclists observed with great interest the ensuing welcoming scenes. They were thinking that someday they too would travel abroad to study or work, as neither a university nor many jobs were available in Cyprus back then.

Soon afterwards, the distinctive siren of the "Fouatie" resounded as the ship entered the harbour, huge clouds of smoke billowing behind it. It was the most renowned ship of the time. The ship sailed the Famagusta-Beirut-Egypt route, carrying crabs, shrimps, palm fruits, and many other delicacies. They turned and looked at Demos. They used to joke that his father was a "Fouatie" on account of his heavy smoking.

The boys entered the old city to complete their ride. "Let's pass by the little lion, for Andreas to complain that Androulla won't fall in love with him," Demos said. And so, once again, they saw the sculpture of the sitting lion, a symbol of mighty Venice.

Walking through the city along with their fellow students, Demos and Andreas and Tourhan too could see several derelict buildings, some of which were evidently churches. Tourhan explained the origin of the Turkish remnants, mostly water springs and baths.

"Apart from religious buildings, they considered water supply and cleaning works particularly important," he added.

They exited from the main gate and ended up at Andreas' orchard for tangerines. Before that, they had passed by Karoullas' pharmacy, near the gate, to have him change the dressing on Tourhan's knee wound. He had fallen down the day before when he and Andreas glided on their bikes, hands outstretched, on the downhill road to the Electricity Plant towards Evagoras Avenue. They were endeavouring to show off their skills to some girls passing by.

Karoullas was dear to the Turks of the old city because "he acted the doctor too," as they used to say; he knew which medicine to prescribe for a cold and other illnesses and he could also dress wounds.

Then came the spring of 1956. Andreas' fellow student, Niki, and her mother accompanied Niki's grandmother outside the walls and walked with her to her house on Larnaka Avenue, near the point where the avenue opened to the big street with Alexandros Demetriou's shops. Demetriou imported "Airmotor" windmills and supplied most of the citrus fruit orchards in Famagusta. On their way back, as they made to pass by the gate near their house, they saw several Turks on the walls yelling "Taksim," which meant partition, in reaction to the Greeks' struggle for union with Greece. As they approached further, they saw that the gate was swarmed with people. It was dangerous to go in. They went back to Niki's grandmother's house and spent the night there. Eventually her family would settle outside the walls, in the Nea Smyrni area.

"How can a minority of 18%, scattered across Cyprus, demand its own territory? How is this possible in the 20th century?" Niki used to wonder.

Not long after, the reaction of the Turks against the prospect of *Enosis* escalated, and one day the mob surged out of the walls to spread fear, kill, and loot. They targeted the few Greek houses and shops nearby in order to displace the people, to chase them away so that they themselves could expand and enlarge their ghetto.

The walls kept the Turks intact. Their religion

and the walls guarded them from assimilation. Within the old city, a sense of ongoing Ottoman rule lingered.

On that day of the attack of the Turks, Andreas was left without a mother. She was killed during the attack. His pain was immense. Sometime after, he would find solace in a beautiful prostitute who had moved from the old city to the Refrigerators Road along with other prostitutes, they too chased by the Turks. Their new road suited them fine, as it served as passage for sailors from the harbour to the new city. It was also a passage for those who went there to buy ice for their coolers.

By then, Andreas had already joined EOKA. When he joined the Executioners, his first two assignments were the execution of British inter-rogators-tormentors. Niki, his fellow student, had been his collaborator. She was the one who had carried the pistol to and from the place of the ex-ecution. Platonic love had grown between them, as dictated by the ethics of the Struggle.

Andreas had never forgotten the day of his moth-er's loss. The bestiality of the Turks had made him ruthless; it was the reason why, after the Struggle, he gave himself to drink and partying and left no challenge unanswered.

The years went by and the coup d' etat came to pass in 1974. During the coup, not a single Turk had been harassed by the Greeks. But when the

Turkish invasion followed, with all the ensuing atrocities, it was only to be expected that animosities broke out across Cyprus, wherever there were Turkish strongholds inside the enclaves they had created themselves in 1963.

Greek Cypriot soldiers and volunteers in Famagusta began operations near the walls, on either side of Larnaka Avenue, and wherever there were Turkish strongholds. Andreas was among the volunteers who attacked, fighting with others to take over a barricaded house whose occupants resisted fiercely. After quite some time, firing from the stronghold ceased. Two emerged, their hands raised in surrender. When Andreas got into the house he saw two slain men. He looked up, as though telling his mother he had lawfully avenged her death. When he turned the slain man who lay prostrate, he recognized his childhood friend, Tourhan, whom he hadn't seen in years. The two captives, who knew of Andreas and his friendship with Tourhan, noticed his sorrow. They pleaded with him and he let them go. Later he found out that Tourhan had been trained in Turkey to become an officer of the Turkish army. Shortly before the invasion he had been deployed in Famagusta.

Responding to the coup d' etat, Turkey invaded Cyprus and conquered Famagusta. All the Greeks and other Christians residing there became refugees. Years later, Demos brought up the subject among his group of friends. "Little did we know that the old city was the fifth column. With its Turkish population and separate structures, shut in and guarded by the surrounding walls, it was a ticking time bomb, a political, geographical, and military time bomb, which eventually exploded and not only shook Famagusta to its foundations but went on to spread over and devour it."

And now the Famagustans can only see their city as servile visitors. Those who didn't reside within and around the old city feel they don't have a special connection to it. In their memories they nostalgically recall the harbour, the walls, Aghios Georgios Exorinos, but not so much its neighbourhoods, not so much its people. Still, it had always been an inextricable part of wider Famagusta, one that cannot be excluded from their remembrance.

Demos' friends and relatives did not expect things would escalate the way they did. They had never imagined that the great democratic forces would endorse, in the last years of the 20th century, the violent movement of populations on the premise of ethnicity. Demos pointed out, "They essentially imposed on us the partition of the island and we went along with it." "If only the same fate befell them," some said. "And, the worst of all is that they made us sign agreements that are bound to lead to the Turkification of the whole of Cyprus,"

Demos insisted. "Not a single modicum of Greekness will be left behind." Others said, "the Turks had prepared everything beforehand, while Greek Cypriots, gullible and unsuspecting as they were, either slept or partied." One proposed, "Why are you so pessimistic? We'll eventually work things out with our Turkish compatriots. We have so much in common."

Andreas didn't want to talk about these things. From the first day of his life as a refugee he closed himself off, until he finally met with his first love. On the night they were to go out to a coastal restaurant with their chosen guests to announce their decision to marry, he went out to the garden of his house, waiting for Niki to get ready. Two shots from very close by struck him. He fell into the jasmine, which sprinkled him with its flowers. Before his soul left his body, he saw Tourhan standing over him with a sarcastic look on his face: so much did Tourhan's son look like his father.

Nobody ever found out who had killed Andreas.

The Chameleon

Katerina was a second-grader at the local elementary school. Every morning before leaving for school she passed by her grandfather's guesthouse that was built within her parents' yard, to say good morning and to take the sandwich he had made for her. Before stepping into her grandfather's house she enjoyed smelling the flowers of the honeysuckle on the fence right opposite his door. She inhaled deeply, as though the exquisite scent would lend her the strength she needed to do well in class. Even though she was an excellent student, she was always nervous. What she wasn't nervous about, however, was getting to school, as she was one of the fastest runners. And when she grew up a bit, she was also very good at ballet and Olympic gymnastics.

One morning as she leant to smell the honeysuckle she came face to face with a lizard. She jumped up, calling for her grandfather. She loved her grandfather dearly. He helped her with her homework and talked to her about their house in Varosi.

As she waited for her grandfather to come, she looked at the lizard basking motionless in the sun. It didn't run away in fear, like other lizards. This particular lizard was different. Hunched up, it had its tail wrapped around a branch.

Her grandfather ran outside to see Katerina pointing to the lizard. He smiled at her tenderly.

"I do think you have heard us talk about the 'ha-molios,' the 'nose-biter.' Well, here it is in the flesh! Its official name is chameleon. Don't be scared! It's not aggressive. Though you shouldn't bring your face or hands close to it, because its jaws are really strong, and once it bites on something it won't eas-ily let go. It could even cut off tender little fingers like yours!"

"Did we have a honeysuckle in our home in Var-osi too?" Katerina asked, eager to learn more about the places that everyone at home talked about.

"Yes, and that too had a chameleon," her grand-father replied with a laugh. He went on to explain that "chameleon" denoted a lion of the ground, one that crawled; and that in the Cypriot dialect it was known as a "nose-biter." Smiling still, he added that once it bit your nose, it would take a donkey mounted on the roof to let you go—or so legend has it.

Katerina was not much of a believer in folk tales, but from that day on, every time she went to her grandfather's she kept a safe distance from the bush that hosted the chameleon. Oftentimes, if she didn't get there on time for her sandwich, her grandfather took it to her at her room. In truth, she wasn't very fond of the sandwich, because most of the time she wasn't hungry. She preferred to save her allowance to buy "Katerina" and other children's magazines instead of spending it on cheese-pies, regardless of how much she liked them. If she didn't eat the sandwich by the afternoon, her grandmother ate it. Refugees threw nothing away. So Katerina, who couldn't even empty her lunch plate, had to put up with everyone mumbling about how she needed to eat and grow stronger.

One day she saw the chameleon on the grey enclosure, and it too was grey. She wasn't puzzled; she had learned from her grandfather that the chameleon changes colours, that it takes on the colour of the surface on which it lies, and that this change of colour serves as camouflage, so that both its enemies and its prey have a hard time spotting it. Nature endowed other lizards with speed, but to the lumbering chameleon it gave the ability to camouflage itself. She learned that the chameleon also changes colour when it runs into danger or in other circumstances.

Further, she learned that "chameleon" is used metaphorically for people who are not firm and honest in their principles, but instead change views depending on the occasion and what is to their best interest. Two of her fellow students sprang to mind, and she placed the chameleon in the same lot.

She observed the chameleon often, although she wasn't intrigued. The chameleon, on the contrary, seemed to look at her benignly. With one eye he looked at Katerina on his side and with the other eye he gazed at a mosquito circling around his other side, ready to snatch it. This is how a chameleon's eyes work. They roll and see things independent of one another.

But the chameleon moved too slowly for Katerina's taste, and, a few days later, she lost interest and stopped observing it. "It's too lazy," she said. "It won't move, not even to find food." She saw it shooting out its tongue like a spring to trap flies. According to her grandfather's explanation, there is some kind of adhesive substance at the tip of its tongue, where flies are trapped if it aims well during the shoot-out.

One day it wasn't there; nor the next days. Could it have crawled down the road and got run over by a car? Or perhaps it just left so that Katerina would once again come nearer to smell the honeysuckle? One thing is certain: Katerina still doesn't like chameleons even if they indulge her.

The Teacher

It was late August. Martha picked up the mandolin to rehearse the two songs she would teach her students at the elementary school in a few days. "It's out of tune, Sotiris."

Her husband took the mandolin and sat outside in the yard to tune it in the freshness of the morning. He didn't have a good voice, as opposed to his wife. But by a quirk of nature, he could tune the mandolin better than her. Laughing, he would say it was all about sharpness of the mind rather than vocal skills.

As he was tuning the instrument, two tomatoes that had grown red on the big tomato plant and three fairly large eggplants caught his eye. He didn't need to look at the pepper plant. Within its thick leafage he would always find the ripe hot peppers that he relished. The other plants were not visible from where he sat. They were planted in the large adjacent plot of land that belonged to the Archbishopric. Within that plot, in a small area that measured three by three meters, they had secured a permit to cultivate vegetables. He also saw the female rabbit crouching down in the cage he himself had made with random planks of wood.

She looked at him in anticipation of the clover she would share with her babies.

The small yard supplemented the family's income and provided their two sons with necessary experience. They learned to dig, plant, water, weed, slaughter, and pluck. And of course, they eagerly observed the growth of plants and animals.

After rehearsing the songs, Martha set out to prepare flashcards for the following day's course. Martha's cards were very popular among the children and her colleagues. She was a calligrapher, and orderly with other things as she was with her writing. She wanted things clean and well-organized. Her family led a beautiful, loving life.

When the EOKA struggle was launched, her elder son joined the high school groups. His parents knew, but said nothing, though each time he was late at night they were concerned. Their concern continued even after his graduation.

One day, a few months after he graduated, he was arrested by the British in his workplace and held in custody without trial. From that moment on, Martha could not easily focus, especially when the following day she was supposed to visit him briefly. Nevertheless, she was able to prepare food for him, as detainees were allowed small portions from their loved ones.

One of her colleagues noticed that at times Martha's mind was elsewhere. She talked to her privately. "I fully understand; you miss your son. At least he's close and you can visit. What can I say?" Martha said nothing. She knew that her colleague's son, a sixteen-year-old boy, studied in a Secondary Education school in England, sent there by his parents to better prepare for the entry exams for British universities. The boy was away from any kind of trouble. Her own son, a top-notch student, was never pressured to go abroad to study after high school. They got him an office job that allowed him to keep contributing to the Struggle, according to his wishes.

The Struggle was eventually over, and her sons completed their studies, got married, and gave her grandchildren. Martha, retired by then, enjoyed singing for the little ones, playing with them, showing them the flashcards she had so dearly saved, and not just for this reason. She relished keeping tokens of remembrance.

She had also kept her correspondence with her husband when, for training reasons, he had had to live abroad for a year. She kept the letters locked in a biscuit box made of sheet metal stored on top of the closet. That box was the most precious item in the house. A correspondence of love! A correspondence of love that endured.

One day a neighbour of hers rang her bell and gave her two of the letters. She had found them in her own yard and, reading the names on the envelopes, realized that they belonged to Martha. Martha checked; the box was not in its usual place. They went onto the roof and found the box; it was broken open, with some of the letters still inside and others scattered across the roof tiles. One of the craftsmen and workmen involved in the renovation of the house over the previous days had done the deed. Probably thinking the sealed box contained money, he took it with him on the roof to open it and steal the money unseen. The wind had blown heavily the previous day, scattering the letters.

On that morning of the 20th of July 1974, when the Turks invaded Cyprus, shooting broke out between the Turks of Famagusta and the National Guard. The fears that had lingered since the 15th of July when the coup took place now came true. Martha took the box with their letters, and along with her husband went to their youngest son's house. The house was much farther than her own from the old city and the Turkish strongholds. Her elder son's family was there too, for the same reason. She felt safe there, but also overwhelmed with concern as the absence of her younger son, who had enlisted when the reserve was called upon to serve, felt even stronger there.

The next morning, the gunfire continued. A bullet flew through the open window, hit the opposite wall and, losing speed because of the distance it had traveled, fell to the ground. The airplanes kept bombarding. The grownups had tucked the three children under the stairs as fear took over. Suddenly, Martha collapsed to the floor and they rushed to her. She wasn't breathing.

They wailed in grief over the unexpected death. The women were hugging one another to come to terms with her loss. The neighbours heard their lamentation and rushed to the house. One of them ran outside to call for a doctor. Another one left to find her elder son who wasn't of draft age and who served in the Civil Defence at the Mantzourio Elementary School. He had showed up at the District Military Command to enlist, but was turned down. They told him they didn't have enough guns for all the conscripts, let alone the volunteers.

The elder son arrived, his face shrouded in anguish, put his arms around his mother on the floor and vainly sought signs of life. He rose to his feet with tearful eyes. At that very moment, a doctor who was Martha's neighbour and who had sought refuge at a house down the road for the same reason as she, stepped in. The doctor confirmed her death. Their last hope vanished. Her sensitive heart had collapsed under the weight of anguish.

They laid her down on the bed, next to the babies' cradles. They had no way of knowing when the gunfire would cease. Her husband and the women lamented her loss without end. The children looked on, sad. Never before had they seen any dead person, let alone their grandmother. They thought she would smile any minute. It was an overwhelming situation, with so many people gathered in so small a place.

Her son laid her in the small van of a relative who lived across the street and, together with his father, drove to the hospital. There she would be placed in the mortuary until the gunfire ceased. He was driving slowly because he couldn't close the van's back door. Martha's legs protruded from the rear; he hadn't been able to bend them, and he was worried lest he dropped her at some turn or uphill road.

The hospital was full of corpses and injured. He was told to go to Markos Hotel, which had been turned into a station for the services he required. But there too, there was no space left. He couldn't come up with any other solution other than to drive her to the Church of the Holy Cross, which had the cemetery in its vicinity. The church was locked. He left his father in the car and walked to the priest's house. There, they told him that the priest was in an orchard along with others. He found him, and they decided to bury Martha in one of the intervals between the air bombardments. He also went to the Mantzourio Elementary School and kindly asked three friends to help him carry the casket.

Martha was buried in a hurry, next to other freshly-dug graves. Within the next few days they added a makeshift wooden cross on the grave, in anticipation of a modest, beautiful monument that would be worthy of her own modesty and beauty.

On the 14th of August, the city was abandoned. People had heard that Turkish tanks had advanced to Famagusta and that an order had been issued to abandon the hospital, which was close to the Turkish strongholds. Martha was abandoned too. She's still waiting for them to put to rest next to her the bones of her beloved husband, who went on to live as a refugee until he too was buried alone in a foreign place.

No one can know whether the cross with her name still stands. Martha is definitely there, among the weeds that have uniformly blanketed all the graves around her, so that no one will be able to tell them apart. She is there, underneath the hot and cold soil, waiting to be found, to listen to the sweet words of her children, her grandchildren and her great grandchildren. Martha, who never had a bad word for anyone, who loved lavishly, who wanted everything to be in harmony, who wanted everything properly done.

Be that as it may, her son, the one who buried her, tells his granddaughter that they will find the grave, and that she shouldn't cry when listening to how they will exhume the bones of the dead and examine them to identify who they belong to. He remembers, he tells her, that his mother's grave lies at the beginning of the row of the tall cypress trees. He also tells her that in springtime they will definitely find it, because amidst the wild mustard flowers, the crown daisies and the mallows, her grandmother's grave will be adorned by those small yellow flowers known to all as tears of Our Lady.

The Sea Scout

Yiakoumis lived outside the walls, but he enjoyed taking strolls in the old city. Oftentimes he would leave his bicycle and climb up the wall at a point where it had crumbled near the old stone-built public water spring. He liked walking along the top of the wall and jumping from embrasure to embrasure. When he reached the point over the port's gate, he would sit down and take in the crowd. He knew the hours and days when each ship entered or left the port. He would glance over at the scene below, letting his gaze travel over the passenger and cargo ships, the travellers, the cranes, the merchandise, the porters; and over the cars too, usually loaded with potatoes and oranges, lined up waiting to unload their goods to be transported by ship, mainly to England.

At the core of his attention he placed the sailors. They would enter and exit the gates in groups. Many of them, passing through the old gate, would go straight to the ladies who worked along the road that ran under the walls, connecting the port's gate to the main gate. The ladies were so great in numbers that when you said, at those times, you would go to Famagusta, some people understood you were going to the ladies. Of course, when the name Famagusta was officially adopted to denote both the walled city of Famagusta and the suburb of Varosha or Varosi, the walled city was called Old Famagusta.

Some sailors would stagger their way back, drunk, any time of the day, depending on their ship's departure time.

Coming back from his stroll, Yiakoumis would sit on the bastion over the main gate, observing passersby along the large street that led to the new city. He could also see carts pausing opposite the gate for the animals to drink water from the troughs there.

On his way down from the wall, he rode his bicycle outside Vasoula's house. They went to high school together, and she lived near the Greek Elementary School of the old city. He wouldn't dare flirt with any beautiful Turkish girl, although there were many of them in the old city, more than the Greek girls.

The Greek elementary school back then had 90 pupils, both boys and girls. The first three classes were hosted in a single classroom with their female teacher, while the last three classes, with their male teacher, shared a different classroom. Vasoula's sister was a first grader. Their family lived opposite the church of St George Exorinos. Because of the port, and seeing that now, under British rule, Greeks were allowed to settle in the old city, as opposed to the prohibition that had applied during Ottoman rule, many Greeks had chosen to live there.

Every Saturday afternoon Yiakoumis put on the blue uniform of the sea scout. That was the day his team assembled. He enjoyed leaving the uniform on and walking about for several hours later. Most of all he liked the sea hat and the band that read "30th Sea Scout Troop." Of course, he did wonder whether there were indeed an additional 29 troops of sea scouts in Cyprus. After all, there were also troops of scouts in khaki, and the first members of the establishment of the 21st troop of scouts hailed from the sea scouts.

Never once did Yiakoumis miss an assembly. After all, their meeting place was not far. They were hosted in an old stone-built shed on the hill with the pine trees behind the police station. Other sheds were near there too. He never found out why they had been built. If you proceeded along the hill in the direction of the walls, you would arrive at the Turkish school.

His troop also met with Turkish sea scouts to play treasure hunt in the area of Othello's tower. The usual hideouts listed in the written instructions included the sculpted lion, the big iron door of the tower, the Lanitis shop, the Greek grocery store, the crevices on the walls, the adjacent church ruins, and anything that had survived the fury of the Turkish cannons when the city was under siege four hundred years ago, and the ensuing destruction and later pillaging of stones, taken for new buildings.

One night, along with his friends, the Turkish sea scouts, he went to the Turkish summer cinema and watched the Greek film "The beauty from Peran."

A boy from his father's village lived with them in their house so that he could attend high school. This boy was a fellow student of Afxentiou, the hero of the Struggle, who visited often. Many times Yiakoumis spoke in awe about his acquaintance with Afxentiou. The two of them also met in the course of the Struggle, when Yiakoumis brought him messages, guns, and other fighters.

Yiakoumis did not stay in Cyprus. He left for Greece in 1957, where he graduated with the rank of captain. Ships had always been his biggest love. For years he would sail first with a commercial ship and then on an oil tanker through the big oceans, away from Cyprus. Some said that the cause of his departure had been an old love of his from the years of his youth. He would often disembark in Buenos Aires, where a cousin of his lived, and in New York, where his wife lived, whom he had married at a ripe age. He also enjoyed docking at the great port of Oakland, California, after sailing under the Golden Gate bridge and across the

Bay of San Francisco. But most of all he enjoyed getting off the ship in Melbourne, where he felt he was on Greek soil. He especially felt this on the great feast-day of the Greek community, when the central street closed in order to accommodate a plethora of stands selling Greek products, drinks, and delicacies, and he relished taking in the scent of souvlaki.

Almost fifty years after the end of his scout's life, and thirty years after the conquest of Famagusta by the Turks, when the roadblocks opened, Yiak-oumis went to see his old house and walk along his old neighbourhoods. He got there at dawn, when everybody was asleep. He didn't wish to come across any of his old Turkish friends; not that he would necessarily recognize them after so many years. Still, he was afraid lest he smile at them, lest he shake their hands as though nothing had happened, as though nothing's happening.

The Magpies

"Here come the magpies," said Lakis, the entertainer of the group of friends. Lakis lived in one of the many orchards in the district of Stavros, in Famagusta, which were typically frequented by magpies. The friends were walking up and down the central street of what was then a small town. They all turned their heads and saw four girls from their school casually riding their bicycles towards them.

"Why on earth would you call those lovely ladies magpies?" Miltis asked. "A magpie is a crow, right?" asked Kostis, a city-dweller, and therefore not knowledgeable about birds. He went on, "What do these young ladies have to do with crows? Crows can only caw and gather in vacant plots rattling harshly at each other. They're ugly birds with pointed beaks. These girls are beautiful."

"A magpie is not the same as a crow," Lakis explained. "Hooded crows are indeed ugly. But if you take a closer look at a magpie, you'll notice how its wings are of a beautiful black colour, white on the neck and breast, a bit like the girls' school uniform. And, what's important of all, they chatter and shake their heads and their behinds like school girls!"

When the girls approached, all the boys smiled at them, each resting his eyes on his favourite one. The girls slowed down a bit, flashed them a quick smile, and carried on. The town's small society left no room for long conversations.

Twenty minutes later, Lakis rode his bicycle to the street behind the municipal grocery store where Yiannoula was waiting, just like she always did after the exchange of smiles on the street. He held her hands and made to kiss her, and she blushed. "Some other time," she protested. The relation was short-lived.

Yiorgoula, who was also a cute girl, caught his eye. That relation lasted longer but they eventually parted ways because of their college studies.

As a college student, Lakis came across girls who were either serious or superficial, beautiful or pleasant enough. Eventually he got married and went on to have children and grandchildren.

Since losing his wife he's been living alone in a suburb of Athens, a refugee away from his birthplace. From his corner apartment on the third floor he has a view of four streets with low-rise apartment buildings and pine trees growing along the pavements. Every morning and afternoon he sits on the large veranda. He is not acquainted with his neighbours not because he doesn't like them. It's just that this is how the world is now. Without focusing too much, he looks at the old lady sitting on the same chair until the sun sets, the young woman who takes her cat on a leash up on the rooftop, and other people, not many. The surrounding buildings are mostly inhabited by lonely people or elderly couples who are only rarely visited by their children and grandchildren. He ponders how much the world has changed.

Then he looks at the birds. It's the first time in his life that he has had the opportunity, living as he does on a level above the trees, to observe their behaviour closely. The sparrows and the pigeons he had always known well. But now he carefully watches the collared doves, searching, according to the myth, for their eighteen children, mournfully repeating the plea 'decaocto.'

He can also see green parrots. One time he counted nine of them coming and going, piercing the air and whistling wildly over the pine trees every morning and every afternoon. He thought that someone kept them in a cage and had let them out for an excursion. He wonders why they return to the cage instead of soaring away. Perhaps they prefer the safety of the cage. Or perhaps a couple of them had escaped from some cage in the area, multiplied, and lived well in Greece as a result of the climate change that impacts the lives of people and birds.

He also sees many magpies. They too take to the air every morning and afternoon. They fly from rooftop to rooftop, from tree to tree; they sit, flick their tails, and their heads with their robust beaks, cawing simply "trrrt," or more eloquently "tate-touta, ta, tou." And again "ta," as though to corroborate what they had just said. Then they set out jumping about for grains.

They might even snatch a gleaming ring, carelessly forgotten somewhere. People say that magpies like shiny little things; they enjoy grabbing shiny trinkets and carrying them to their nest. They have been famous for this. Both an opera and a novel are titled "The Thieving Magpie."

So they are thieves, with ugly beaks, dressed in black, garrulous, and with a preference for jewels; and still so vibrant, delightful, very sociable, very necessary.

Lakis waits for the magpies every morning and every afternoon. He has the notion they talk to him. He doesn't respond; he wouldn't like his neighbours to think he's crazy.

At a meeting, quite some time ago, in a friendly tavern with his old school buddies, Miltis and Kostis, who had come from Cyprus with a bottle of zivania, he told the story of the same magpies frequenting the rooftop, the antennas, and the solar heaters of every apartment building; to be exact, how each magpie frequented the same apartment building. On the oldest building, the magpie spoke and flicked its head and tail in the manner of

Yianoula. On another building, in the manner of Yiorgoula. But on other apartment buildings too, the voices and motions sounded familiar. He had had just a little bit too much to drink, just like old times. They took him to his apartment and, even though it was nearly midnight, Lakis thought he heard magpies, when the only voice echoing was the monotonous and grieving call of the sole re-maining scops owl in the area. "Kweeoh!" And then again, "Kweeoh."

He left a name, Lakis did, for loving and enjoy-ing, both as a youth and as an old man, magpies dressed in black with white collars, whether they had good or bad names, whether they were lasses or birds.

The Captain

"Up on the belfry again?" the priest shouted at him. "Get down quickly or I'm not going to let you hold the cherubim icons."

Markos lived near the church. After school he played with the other kids in the churchyard. On days when the others didn't come, he liked climbing up the belfry to gaze at the blue sea, barely a mile away, or at the green vastness of the orange trees of Aghios Memnon and Kato Varosi.

The children loved the priest, but they also had their own ways. They played loudly and argued, and annoyed the neighbours at noontime.

In the winter they loved riding their bicycles along the dirt roads between the orange orchards, stopping now and then to enjoy oranges and tangerines. They thought it was only natural to pick the fruit, and so did the owners of the orchards! In the summer they had their eyes on the figs. They knew where to find the best fig trees. Only rarely would someone chase after them, and only in the event that they broke a branch or ruined a fence.

By the time he went to high school, Markos had stopped climbing up the belfry. Some afternoons he would be at the stadium, because the school's gymnast had picked him to train in jumping, especially the triple jump. The summers he would spend by the sea.

One day in twelfth grade, a few months after he had joined EOKA, when his father suspected his son's involvement, Markos told him: "These are just small-time ventures. I want to become an officer of the Greek Army."

He followed the usual path of professional army officers: Military Academy, then service in Macedonia, in the Royal Guard, and in Cyprus, where he was secretly deployed along with other Cypriot officers.

When the Junta seized power, the Cypriots were summoned back to Greece. "If they've summoned us back, then they're up to something," Markos would say over and over again. In the end, however, they demobilized him, and he returned to Famagusta.

When the Turkish invasion was launched, he was living in Famagusta as a civilian and so had to ask for permission to rejoin the army. There was no objection to his participation in the defence. Everyone was required. He took over a company in the southern foothills of Pentadaktylos, where he had previously served. He knew all the residents of the surrounding villages. The soldiers serving in the company were the children he had often seen in the village, greeting him respectfully when he ran into them with their parents in houses, the coffee-shop, or in the street.

During the first battles he lost six men. He didn't have enough weapons to engage with the fully equipped Turks. On the night of the day when the Turkish tanks advanced to their front line of trenches on the mountains, he admitted it was impossible for them to stand their ground. He attached a Beretta pistol to his belt along with a .38 Smith and Wesson revolver, his weapons of choice, and set out for inspection, a Thompson hanging over his shoulder.

"We'll get them tomorrow, Captain, sir!" exclaimed the guard in the northern trench with a military salute. He was one of those kids he had known. The guard had lost his father, who had fought with a group of volunteers.

Also keeping guard in the southern trench was another one of those boys who had believed the rumours that Greek aircrafts were on their way, or that the following day they would be supplied with heavy equipment, most importantly with anti-tank RR, and that cannons would soon arrive to strike and to create a safety zone. The boy himself was the son of an ironsmith who used to make grenades with water pipes during the EOKA struggle. He followed his father's vocation. He carried one of the two Bren guns of the company. "Are the RR coming tomorrow, sir? I want one!"

"We'll see," Markos replied. "Are you familiar with the RR?"

"Yes sir! Recoilless Rifle!"

Markos walked on and sat on the ground behind a bush that was moist with the nocturnal dew that had settled, as always, upon the plain of Mesaoria. There was no help on the way. The major had been very clear. "Tomorrow all these children will perish," Markos thought to himself. "Their dreams are gone. They are willing to sacrifice their lives for the homeland. But for treason? Must they sacrifice themselves for the Junta's treasonous plans?"

He had always had this fear, that the Junta had been preparing something atrocious; but not calamity of this scale! It was past midnight when he made up his mind. He immediately ordered the soldier who had lost his father, the soldier whose father was unfit to work, another soldier and another one to retreat under cover of darkness along a designated remote line. To the lieutenant he said that he had a plan in mind. And so he managed to send several boys away with specific orders. As for him, he stayed back with quite a few others. He had to perform his duty. Before dawn, an order from the major instructed them to retreat. He wasn't pleased. He had prepared himself for the ultimate battle.

In Larnaka, where he would settle for the following years, now and then he ran into some of his soldiers. They respected him as always.

A few years later he was transferred to Greece. He wasn't young when he got married. He and his wife only stayed together for a few years. 'Irreconcilable differences' was their version of the story.

When he retired from service, he lived in Porto Rafti, Greece, in a cottage with an orchard. He was content in the company of trees and birds, away from ceremonies and scheming army officers. "Trees and birds can't speak, so they can't lie," he would mutter over and over again. He even sold fruit to the grocer nearby, to add to his meagre pension that wasn't enough for him to make ends meet and to help those in need around him, as he wished to do.

Only two things did he miss: halloumi and commandaria wine. Eventually he would find halloumi from a Cypriot refugee, a woman from Yialousa who had settled in Markopoulo and made halloumi to sell. Commandaria was the only thing he would gladly accept from friends who visited from Cyprus. Perhaps he liked it so much because, in drinking it, he relived the years that the priest allowed him a sip if there was any left over in the bottle. Any commandaria left in the holy grail, after the Holy Communion, the priest had to drink himself.

He liked walking by the small bay of Porto Rafti with the fishing boats and the taverns. There was one particular tavern where he liked to sit and eat fresh fish and cephalopods. He relished cephalopods, especially sun-dried octopus. So many of them were hanging in the sun at the seaside, just like back at the Famagusta Nautical Club near Aghia Triada. He had gone there often in the days of his youth.

He didn't want to return to Cyprus, not even for a mere visit. "What am I supposed to do there?" he would say. "Cry out that they've lost their faith in Hellenism? That they've lost their Greekness? That they no longer call themselves Greeks but Grecocypriots? That they've lost their primordial principles? No, I have no business going back there."

Then the time came when sickness sent him to the hospital. Even there, he would always share a joke and advice. In the end he couldn't withstand successive surgeries.

It was a solemn funeral service. The casket, draped with the Greek flag, was carried under the honorary arch of swords. Nobody could see whether Markos was smiling inside the casket with that ironic smile of his at having to endure the official ceremony. But he definitely must have smiled contentedly when his true friends and patriots wept.

The Immigrant

"If you want to try and see if you like being a mechanic, come back on Monday morning. I will pay you one shilling a day. Does your father agree with this?"

"He does. All right, thank you," Stamatis told Prastitis, one of the finest car mechanics in Famagusta. In fact, Prastitis was the sales representative of Javelin cars.

Stamatis, fourteen at the time, was the son of Theodosis, the owner of the area's coffee house, and both he and his younger siblings did chores there after school. Prastitis had appreciated the boy's eagerness and politeness, and rightly so.

At the coffee house Petros took over as first assistant, however without giving up the right to joke around one way or another. One time, his father caught him writing something down.

"At Barclays they're waiting for their coffee and you're scribbling away? What are you writing there?"

Theodosis snatched the piece of paper and saw a list of customer names on it.

"What's this list, boy?"

"Fussy customers."

There was a wild look in Theodosis' eye but he let

his son carry on. "This one wants his coffee bubbly and so I must pour it into the cup from high up. This one here wants it in a thick cup. And this one wants his coffee with plenty of froth..."

Petros refrained from saying names lest those sitting near would hear him. But Theodosis was unabashed by the customers. He unbuckled his belt and started spanking the boy with it.

"This one is for this customer, this one is for the other one..." until he finally simmered down. Petros didn't mind. He had been well-trained to enjoy practical jokes even at the cost of being belted.

Not many months had passed since the family moved to the city from Aghios Serghios. Jobs were becoming fewer and fewer in the village and the boys had to go to high school. Stamatis had already been a high school student for two years, staying with relatives in the city. The three girls didn't need to go to high school.

Theodosis ran a coffee house in his village, but he did other jobs too. You see, it was a small village and there was no way it could have one man for every different trade. And to travel to Famagusta would take almost all day. The bus only went there once a day. It left in the morning, carrying mostly workmen, and drove back in the afternoon. Although many made the journey on bicycle, this was more challenging during the summer or winter.

One of the trades that Theodosis took on was

that of comb-maker: he made weaving combs for looms. He started with unprocessed reeds and delivered artistic combs. Again, the boys were his helpers. They had learned how to make the 'samaja,' the slender reed dividers between the threads, and tie them to the two 'vaines,' the small slender rods they would make with big stems from the leaves of palm trees. For every thirty-five 'samaja' they would add five coloured ones, so that the weaving woman could easily estimate how many and which threads to draw through the warp. Forty 'samaja' on the weaving comb comprised a 'thilidji,' a loop ten centimetres in length.

When Stamatis began making combs of ten 'thilidjia' each, he asked his father to start paying him. "Your pay covers your high school tuition," Theodosis told him, casting so critical an eye on him that he almost dipped the razor into the cheek of the man he was shaving! He was a barber, too! Thankfully he managed to complete the man's shaving without further trouble.

"Theodosis, I can't stand this toothache. I've been on aspirin since yesterday and it still won't go away. Come pull it out," a fellow villager exclaimed, rushing in. Theodosis put the razor aside and pulled the forceps out of the drawer, sterilized it on the small blue spirit stove, and set about pulling the tooth out. The tooth had deep roots, and so the ailing man had to help, holding Theodosis' hand firmly and pulling along with him to dig out the tooth. Theodosis gave him salt water to rinse his mouth with.

No sooner had he completed that task than a boy came in yelling: "My grandma said you must hurry there and let her blood out because she's feverish."

"Go on, I'll be right there." Theodosis was certified by Dr Solononidis of Varosi as an expert in tooth extraction and bloodletting, and the framed certificate hung prominently on the wall of the coffee-shop. He took the fleam, the bloodletting instrument, out of the drawer and ran. When he got there he found the old woman seated on a comfortable chair out in the yard. On another chair, which had a towel spread over its backrest, she had rested her left arm, her sleeve rolled up. After tying her arm over the elbow to make the veins pop out, Theodosis lit the blue spirit stove and sterilized the fleam, and then with a careful, quick motion cut open the vein right in the middle of the hand. Blood sprang out in a curve before dyeing the ground red. On other occasions, when the bloodletting was done inside, they would have a bowl under the chair. The old lady was moving her fingers to help ease the blood out.

"There's lots of work today, but I'm afraid this is rarely the case," he would later tell his customers at the coffee house. "That's why I'm leaving for the city." And that's exactly what he did. Luckily, his wife had inherited a house in the city from her father.

There he set up a coffee house and quit the comb-making trade, as women had stopped weaving. His income from the coffee house was not enough. Most of it came from the owners and employees of the surrounding stores, offices, and workshops. In wintertime several customers frequented the coffee house. But in the summer it was hot inside, while outside in the yard only a few could tolerate the stench of horse droppings from the horse-drawn carts that waited right outside the coffee house to pick up those who had work to do in other parts of the city.

Everything his daughters earned, he let them keep them for their dowry. The girls were seamstresses among other things. They also made tapers and wreaths for weddings and funerals. They had even set up a sign outside their house advertising their services.

Eventually, to make ends meet, he decided to start making coffee house products in his own house. With the help of his wife and children he roasted and ground coffee beans, roasted whole peanuts with plenty of salt, and made lemonade. All these things, along with loukoumia and other foodstuff for coffee houses, which he would buy at wholesale prices, he loaded into an old green van of his, driving around the villages to sell it to other coffee house owners. The competition was intense. Eventually the big companies prevailed and Theodosis had to make do with his own coffee house. But even though he supplied a large area of stores near him, his net income did not suffice.

In the meantime, Stamatis grew up to be a good mechanic. But the idea got into his head that he would have a better life if he moved to Australia. A travel agent was promoting an upcoming journey to Australia for emigrants. He went there and paid the ticket in advance, but time passed and the prospective emigrants were still waiting to hear about their journey. All together they went to the agency to protest that they had been cheated out of their money. The travel agent then went to Italy and chartered an old ship. He did some renovations on it and sailed it to the port of Limassol. Back then, most passenger ships sailed to either Limassol or Larnaka, while most cargo ships traveled to Famagusta.

The "Corsica" finally departed for Australia on 17 December 1951 with 1080 passengers on board, 800 Greeks of Cyprus and 280 Greeks from Greece. Many of them were travelling with their families.

The ship gave them a good breakfast, but the steaks and other dishes served for lunch were hardly edible. Because no dinner was served on board, they had to save part of their lunch for the night. As for water, they bought it at two shillings per bottle.

After replenishment in Djibouti, the ship set out to sail for Colombo, Ceylon. Before they got there, a terrible stench wafted all over the ship. The potatoes and onions loaded into the depths of the ship in Limassol to be unloaded in Colombo had gone bad. But because they also served as ballast, they couldn't dump them into the sea for fear that the ship wouldn't stay balanced. They offloaded them in Colombo and loaded a different ballast. After a total of 51 days they finally arrived in Melbourne, having first stopped for a little in Perth.

Along the way Stamatis made the acquaintance of many people. He mostly kept company with Yiorgos from Deryneia, Sophocles from Paralimni, and Antonakis from Aghios Memnon. He also read the only book he had taken with him aside from his Greek-English and English-Greek dictionary. The book was *Romantic Cyprus* by Kevork Keshishian. It had been a gift from the Turkish bookseller next to Prastitis, so that he wouldn't forget about Cyprus.

Stamatis got a job in Melbourne and habitually wrote his news to his family. Everyone back home began envisioning themselves in the big city that provided work and good remuneration.

Four years later, Theodosis' entire family had had their credentials for emigration to Melbourne assessed and they had been accepted for emigration. As the day of departure drew closer, the upheaval of choosing what to pack grew bigger and bigger. They left at dawn, went to Limassol, made it to the pier, and boarded the boat that took them to the "Kyrenia." They leant on the rail and looked toward the land, taking in everything they would only dream about for several years to come.

A few years later, Stamatis' three fellow travelers married his three sisters. The emigrants were supporting each another in their new country, just like the people in their villages back home, in and around Famagusta, had supported each other.

Stamatis or Stam, as he came to be known in Melbourne, and his wife, Angeliki or Angie, and his brothers visited Cyprus several years later. Some of the brothers even returned three or four times, bringing along some of their children, those who could speak some Greek and were intrigued by their parents' homeland.

Sixty years after their emigration, Theodosis' family, including sons-in-law and daughters-in-law, numbered more than 100 members.

Two years after Stamatis lost his wife he visited Cyprus again with his daughter Kyriakoula or Keny. His wife had made him promise that on his next journey he would take Kyriakoula with him. It was the first time that Kyriakoula, by that time forty-two years old, had been to Cyprus. She was excited. She went everywhere, taking pictures all the time. She had heard so much about this homeland! She was particularly happy to meet her second cousins again. These cousins had gone to Australia with their parents, refugees from Famagusta, and had stayed there for many years but had eventually returned home.

Stamatis was sitting with his cousins in a restaurant by the sea of Protaras when a mobile phone rang and he heard one cousin saying on the phone, "We're with the Australians." When he hung up, he told them "That was Maroula. She sends her best." Then Stamatis said: "In Cyprus we're Australians, in Australia we're Greeks!"

When it was time to leave, Stamatis rose to his feet and walked to the edge of the natural plateau in Protaras. He stood there for a long time, gazing at the sea, the tourists swimming or lying under autumn's sun, the vast sandy beach with countless hotels. And then, closing his eyes, he saw the sea extending to occupied Famagusta, the occupied beach of Salamis which for him was also the beach of Aghios Serghios, and then beyond, until he heard his cousin's voice: "Haven't you had enough of gazing? It's time to go." "Come join me in relishing," Stamatis replied. And they relished.

"Will I get to see Famagusta again?" Stamatis wondered aloud to his cousin. His eyes were moist, perhaps from the sun.

Kyriakoula approached and heard his words.

"Come on, papa, let's go. We're late."

"Let's go, Keny."

The Cities

It was a matter of a few more lines, and the city he had designed on the computer would be ready for submission to the international competition announced by the Competent Authority of Spain. The city was designed to be built on the island that had emerged from the sea off the Spanish shores some time ago, just like another island had emerged off the coast of Japan earlier. But this particular island was much larger. It was almost the size of Cyprus.

He had decided that the city intended to be the island's capital would be coastal. He had studied the history and culture of that area of Spain, and had gone there to see the public and private buildings, the life of the residents, and also the natural landscape, as a similar landscape was expected to take shape on the new island.

Lefteris had specialized in designing cities, and right from the start he was concerned about one thing. Who would inhabit this city, and which trades would they engage in? "History tells us that many cities have been built from scratch. The Competent Authority will decide," he pondered.

He had made provision for the residences, the squares, administrative buildings, schools, theatres, commercial streets, industrial zones, supermarkets, and parks. It was up to the Authority to decide on the rest; the competition announcement included no further reference.

Everything had been arranged. He leaned back in the chair and closed his tired eyes. He had been working from six in the morning and it was already past midnight.

He saw a child facing backwards in the back seat of a car that drove the family away from Famagusta; a six-year-old boy, eyes wide open with fear, looking at the city that was drawing further away. Here and there the city was burning, smoke rising to the sky from scattered fires. He could see the Turkish airplanes approaching, dropping bombs and leaving. In the front seat, his mother drove next to his grandfather. In the back seat, his grandmother held his baby sister in her arms. He had never forgotten that day: 14 August 1974.

The bombers had closed in again two hours earlier. His father had been called to active duty. His mother waited no longer. She picked up what was necessary for the baby and they left for Kokkinochoria, the southern villages. She didn't change clothes; the thought didn't even cross her mind. She left with her short pants, expecting they would seek refuge somewhere for a few hours until the bombing stopped, and then go back. Everyone thought that the Turks only wanted the old city, as none of them lived to its south, not even in Kokkinochoria. They stopped at Deryneia and sat at a coffee house to drink water and tend to the baby. They couldn't stay there long; the place was overflowing with people, voices, and crying. The airplanes came back. They left for Ormideia, where they had relatives. The next day they returned and tried to enter the city in order to take clothes and food from their homes, but in Deryneia they saw the National Guard departing in an orderly fashion.

In the house that took them in, some thirty people, women and children, slept next to each other. The men slept in cars or under the grapevine. They were among the lucky ones. Thousands of others slept under carob trees and olive trees.

The siren of a fire truck awoke him. He was relieved. He went on working for a bit and then, feeling sleepy, he closed his eyes again.

He saw the municipal park in front of the Gymnasium, decorated with orange fruit crafts for the Orange Festival. He saw himself posing in front of the orange-clad dolphin next to the pond. He also saw the sandy beach, with its array of hotels, and then moved on to the free areas of the Famagusta district, so close to the city. He stood for a while in Aghia Napa, where his family camped in the summer during the first years after they became refugees. These were the only vacations they could afford, and that was also the only way they could spend a few days in these areas where they used to take him as a little boy. He could even see the list he had so eagerly put together back then in the tents, with every new restaurant, every new cafeteria, every new hotel and apartment complex sprouting fast, one after the other, inside and around the otherwise virgin areas, weaving the fabric of a new small town. How lucky, the non-refugees! After the fourth year he stopped adding to the list. It wasn't worth it anymore. By contrast, imprinted indelibly on his mind were the orange orchards and the fields and the seaside places on the verge of extinction. So much had he loved them!

His parents and sister had stayed in the tent with him. Their own tent and the one next to it, which hosted a couple, family friends, they had set up themselves under a carob tree at a short distance from the sea, near a seaside restaurant from which they bought water. They had even made a small makeshift kitchen with two tables and impromptu cabinets.

One day an aunt paid them a visit. As the aunt

sat in the shadow of the carob tree the little girl, his sister, grabbed her hand and whispered softly, "Come see. Come quickly!" She even gestured to her to keep quiet. They walked slowly and carefully toward a small bush. "Did you see? Did you see the cut-tail?" She pointed to a lizard with its tail cut off, running to and fro. It would stop, raise its head, look left and right, and then speed up again as though chasing something or being chased after. Then it would crawl into a hole and after a while crawl out. It was the girl's favourite among many lizards in the area. You could see their tracks upon the thin sand, drawing all sorts of shapes. There were also snakes in the vicinity, but they were less scared of them because their tent was sealed with a zipper and because they had put garlic and small stones around it.

The aunt had spent the night with them. The following day it was Lefteris' turn to call to their aunt, "Come see!" He showed her his collection of shells in a large cardboard box, proudly demonstrating his triton, which he had found upon lifting a large stone on the seabed. He also had two 'cypraeas,' the shells with which farmers used to adorn their bags, or 'vourkes,' hanging the shells on thin leather belts. The children had dubbed the shells, too, 'vourkes.' Within a few days, the aunt bought her own tent and set it up next to them.

One night as they were lying down ready to sleep they had noticed a light flickering. From the tent's window that was covered in tulle, they saw it was the turn signal of the car that belonged to the residents of the adjacent tent. They were certain someone had tried to break into the car. Their friend approached but found the car locked. When he opened it to switch off the signal, a mouse jumped right out. As they realized the next day, the mouse had eaten his way through a piece of rubber that sealed off a hole in the underbelly of the car and, strolling around, had climbed onto the turn signal switch, turning it on.

They were still talking about it at lunch while eating the small wrasses that Lefteris had caught. He had used a plastic bottle which he cut in half, reinserting the inverted top half of the bottle into the bottom part like a funnel so as to operate like a 'skarka' fish trap. For bait he had used urchin flesh. He would detach the urchins from the rocks with a long, pointed knife. He didn't much like fish, but wrasses, though not particularly tasty, he ate willingly. They were his achievement. He even liked limpets, which were all the more rare to find. Later they would all learn that they shouldn't collect live shells and clams because their population was decreasing and some species were in danger of extinction.

Once again Lefteris opened his eyes, thinking that he must make provision in his design for seaside camps for children, as well as for ports for fishermen, even though at this stage of the competition such details were not necessary.

He leaned back again. He saw their new home being built a few years later in the city where they had fled; the search for a plot of land and talks about the arrangement of the house. "Odd how each person's conditions of life impact their professional choices!" he thought, as he had many times before.

He vaguely remembered Famagusta, but couldn't tell which part of his recollections came from his own true memories and which from the narration of his parents and other relatives. Eventually, he had built up inside him his own Famagusta, his birthplace, his city, just like it was back then; though today the city is shorn of residents, and his own family home in ruins.

Through the years he visited other cities across the world, as a student or a tourist, as a Professor of Architecture or to participate in conferences, or even to accompany his students during a special semester he had designed himself, titled "Cities of the Mediterranean." The course included a few days' visit to a coastal city. So far over the previous semesters he and his students had traveled to Venice, Athens, Rome, Marseilles, Barcelona, Alexandria, Thessaloniki, Corfu, Pafos, Volos. He had to be aware of everything, old and new buildings, the way of life, the culture, to be able to explain to his students the relation between buildings and the people that lived in and around them, so that they could better sketch the White Tower, the Parthenon, Gaudi's Sagrada Familia, Fontana di Trevi, and countless other buildings. Each city became his own, just like its residents, their lives. Cities, cities, cities. And Famagusta?

His eyes closed again. And he saw it. The new Famagusta. Sandy, fragrant, laborious, gentle. Brimming with people. His first city.

He sprang up. There's a good exercise for his students! They can see it on their computer via google maps, just like the Famagustans look at it, torn down and full of weeds, as they sit on their sofa and google their home on the laptop. He will ask them to restore the city; or better yet to renovate it and write down what kind of life they think it will acquire; which language the silent city will speak.

"Let's see," he pondered, "whether they will be able to maintain at least some of its most distinctive characteristics. Let's see if they can give her back its voice; its voice of old, the voice I hearkened to as a little boy; the voice exuding from the

lilies of-the-shore, from the centuries-old harbour,
from the sandy beach of Glossa, from the family homes, from the Town Hall, from the Orange
Festival, from the Hellenic Gymnasiums!"

Dimitris Leventis was born to Cypriot parents in Athens in 1939, and grew up in Cyprus. He studied Greek Philology at the University of Athens and Counselling at the State University of New York at Albany. He taught at the First Gymnasium of Famagusta until the Turkish invasion in 1974. He has also worked for and shaped the Counselling Services in Secondary Education in Cyprus. He has published, in Greek, the books *Counselling in Secondary Education* (Nicosia: Epiphaniou, 2004), *Panos Leventis: Poems, Short Stories, Plays* (Nicosia: M. A. Michaelides, 2007; ed.), *The Life and Death of Petros Yiallouros* (Nicosia: 2009), *The Course of the Greek Gymnasiums of Famagusta from 1955 to 1974* (Nicosia: Association of Alumni and Friends of the Greek Gymnasiums of Famagusta, 2013) and *Stories of Famagusta* (Athens: Iolkos, 2015). For the latter publication he was awarded the National Short Story Prize of the Republic of Cyprus.